THE STUNNER

"Behind every strong woman ⸻
that gave her no other choice"

Saron Leila

xx

This book is a work of fiction. Names, characters, organisations, places, events and incidents are either products of the author's imagination or are used fictitiously.

1

Colin J Galtrey
AUTHOR

THE STUNNER 4

Book number four in the highly acclaimed Stunner series by Peak District Author Colin J Galtrey.

The beautiful Saron embarks on her latest journey in life ably supported by her best friends Julie and Helen.

Read how a good turn for a friend throws her into a dangerous life of living on the edge.

This series has a massive following and initially was going to be a one-off book but due to popular demand, was created into a trilogy but, yet again, another book was requested, hence book number four in the series. Go with Saron if you dare, would you be brave enough to do the things she does to survive?

THE STUNNER 4

Chapter 1

In life, we all have ups and downs but my life feels like one long game of Snakes and Ladders and whoever is throwing the dice seems to like finding me all the snakes!

There was a big year coming up for me, Julie and Helen, the big four "O". The London girls came to see us about every two months or we would go up to London.

Things have changed a fair bit since we last spoke, not only had three years passed but Julie had split with Gustav and Helen turned up with her suitcase three weeks later at my doorstep and announced she had left her husband.

THE STUNNER 4

There is some bad news but Julie was a while telling me so I will fill you in when the time is right, which it isn't now.

So, my little cottage was full once again with Julie and Helen both now staying but I wasn't complaining, I loved having my best mates to stay.

We had a couple of bottles of red. Helen was being quite boisterous, when the alcohol began to hit Julie, she broke down. "What is it mate"?

"My little girl, Gustav has taken her, he said I will never see her again. I think he has taken her to Russia". "He won't have Ju, surely not. How old is she now"? "Almost four, she is beautiful" and she passed a picture out of her bag to show me and Helen.

"I don't want to pry but why did you split"? "Well, initially he said it was because I was working all the time but then I found a letter from a woman in London, he had been working down there for about four months and he had been sleeping with her". "Well, maybe he has taken Ezlynn down there". "I just have this feeling that he will be in Russia".

"Look, let's find this woman's address and go down and find out". "Can I say something girls"? Helen said, filling her glass from the third bottle of wine. "My husband had been playing around and I never want to see the cockroach again and please, never say his name to me, I want to forget about the whole bloody episode in my life".

THE STUNNER 4

It made Julie and Saron laugh, Helen had never changed, she always called a spade a spade. It was good to have all my besties together in one place. I have loads to tell you, some good some bad but, hey, that's the life of Saron, as you well know.

Because the wine was flowing, Helen said we should have dinner in Fowey. I wasn't sure that was a good idea. There was just one little boat to take us across to Fowey and with-it being January, everywhere was quiet with just a few hardy folks mingling about, some holidaymakers and some locals.

"Whoop, come on singlets, let's get into The Ship". Helen was on a bender and we all know what can happen, it will be tears before bedtime as mum would say.

THE STUNNER 4

The pub was quite busy, Ju was quiet
which worried me but Helen more than
made up for her. She decided she would
challenge some random guy sat with his
sheepdog to an arm-wrestling
competition. The guy just couldn't stop
laughing. "Well, if you won't take up the
challenge then you have to buy me a
drink". The guy was still laughing when
he went to the bar with Helen looking
after Brian his sheepdog. Helen was
trying to get it to do tricks, it really was
hilarious. She really was a breath of fresh
air. Ju was quiet and I knew she was
thinking about her little girl.

"Ju, we will go tomorrow, we will get
Ezlynn back for you mate". She squeezed
my hand tightly. "It was never right what

Gustav did you know? I will straighten this out".

Back at the cottage, I had a quiet word with Helen, I told her Julie had a breakdown in Scotland but she wasn't to ask about it and we had to find a way of getting Ezlynn back or I was scared she might end up in that dark place again.

Helen was a caring girl and a strong person and if anybody could help, she could. Armed with the address of Gustav's bit on the side, as Helen called her, we headed to London and Canal Apartments in Camden Lock. As you know, Camden Lock is always busy with tourists but they had built some apartments across the lock, very nice indeed, the woman Suzanna Belling lived in Apartment Trafalgar.

We found the door and Helen rang the doorbell; I was convinced she was going to slap the woman when she opened the door but a little guy about seven opened it. "Is mummy in"? I said. The little boy ran down the hall to get his mum. A striking woman in an orange cowl necked jumper and jeans came. "Can I help you"? "Are you Suzanna Belling"? Helen said in an aggressive manner. I decided it was best I stepped in. "Yes, I am, who are you"? "My name is Saron, this is Helen and this is Julie, the wife of Gustav". "I'm sorry, this is bad mannered of me, please come in".

THE STUNNER 4

Over a glass of red wine each, she told us she had been seeing Gustav for about four months but he always said he was single, then, the other week he appeared with a little girl, he said she was his daughter but her mother wasn't looking after her.

"We had a massive row, he had lied to me, now you tell me he was married to you, I am so sorry, I would never have entertained him if I had known and that you had the little girl together". Julie nodded.

"Where is he now"? "He got what few clothes he had left here and said he would never come back and he left". "Do you know where his grandma lives"? "Yes, he spoke often about her".

"Where does she live"? "Just a minute I have a card from her, she sent it to Gustav on his birthday, I think she said this was her address. I didn't think much at the time but maybe he was planning to go there. Here it is, her name is Yolanda Skarage and this is her address, 19 Borossna Apartments, Moscow. I'm sorry, this is all I have and please believe me, I didn't know he was married".

I thanked her, I could tell Helen wanted to knock her block off, Julie said nothing and we left. I truly believed Gustav had hoodwinked her like he had Julie. I had three missed calls from the solicitor in Cornwall but he can wait, we need to get Ezlynn back with Julie, I could tell she wasn't right, she was going back into her shell again.

THE STUNNER 4

I arranged for a direct flight to Moscow for the three of us, here we go again, another bloody adventure! Guess I'm one of those people that likes the excitement of all this.

"Right girls, we'd best go shopping for some warm clothes, my treat". "Saron, you are so kind". "Helen, you and Ju are my best mates and I'm hardly on the bread line so let's go and get three Canada goose parkas, they will keep us warm".

The following day the girls looked like Scott of the Antarctic as they boarded the plane bound for Moscow and the unknown.

As per usual, the girls hit the vodka which really wasn't a good idea, luckily, they had booked a couple of nights in a hotel in Moscow. By the time they got in the concourse poor Ju was the worse for wear, I was feeling a bit squiffy and Helen was up for throwing the bags in the room and finding a bar. I couldn't let her go on her own, seriously, that was the only reason, well, that's my excuse and I'm sticking to that.

We settled Ju in her room, the rooms were like something from 1940's Britain, there were no fancy rooms here. I had a quick wash and the towels were like sandpaper. We were certainly roughing it on this trip. The guy on reception was a bit like Danny DeVito, he had spilt something down his green sweatshirt that was so ill-fitting his large belly looked like it was going to explode any minute and he was one of those creepy guys, looking me and Helen up and down. Helen asked where the best bars were, he came from behind his desk and grabbed my arm while placing his hand on Helen's bottom showing us where to go. It didn't bother Helen, she couldn't stop laughing.

We ended up in a bar called Treacle Creek, a Yank just after the war had owned it, he had married a Russian girl and he wanted a bit of home in Russia hence the Turtle Creek.

Like all the bars in Russia, from what I have been told, they are smoky places and Turtle Creek was no exception. Helen, in her formidable style, ordered "Two of what you people drink"!! The barman looked a bit bemused but grabbed a bottle of Lukinza. I could see two good looking guys watching our every move, eventually they asked us to join them. They ordered more Lukinza then introduced themselves they said they worked in the Swedish Embassy, the one that took a shine to me was called Arvid and his friend, chatting to Helen, not that he could get a word in, was called Nils.

Arvid told me that Russia could be dangerous, I had said we were visiting our friend Julie's family but she had gone back to the hotel. I didn't say poor Ju was hammered because of Helen the beer monster. She had taken Nils dancing and I was having a really nice night. Arvid was a nice guy, quite tall with blonde hair, quite long, in the Robbie Savage style, probably somebody I wouldn't normally have taken a second glance too but he was really nice,

He told me that he lived fifty miles out of Stockholm in a little area called Grolshen, he said the nearest neighbour to him was twenty miles away and his log cabin had the most spectacular views. He was obviously very proud of his cabin. I noticed he had this slightly annoying habit of drumming on the table with his index finger. It was driving me mad so I had to ask him to stop. He apologised and said he didn't know he was doing it but he only did it when he was nervous. "Why are you nervous"? "Because you are beautiful", he said.

I must admit, I did blush at that. Some seventies disco music came on and he asked me to dance. I had on a green dress belted at the waist and some Kurt Geiger brown ankle boots. To be honest, I felt sexy as hell as I danced with this Swedish hunk. We must have danced to about ten songs and it was coming to the end of the night as the DJ started to slow things down. It had been ages since I felt this good.

Arvid held me close and lightly kissed my shoulders and bare neck. He was so sensuous, I felt trembly with anticipation as his body held me tightly. Eventually, we went back to our table. Helen was putting on her coat and announced she would see me at breakfast. I was thinking I hope Arvid asks me back to his apartment. I could see he was a shy guy and if we were going to spend the night together it would be at my suggestion.

Come on Saron go for it, what the hell, you are single, I kept saying to myself as he helped me on with the big warm Canada Goose parka. I just blurted it out, "Shall I come back to yours"? the poor guy stumbled his reply, "Yes, yes, that would be nice".

Too right, buster, I thought. We walked through Moscow with the fresh carpet of white snow crunching under our feet. We arrived at the Embassy, which was probably, at the most, eight hundred yards from my hotel.

His apartment was very tidy for a bloke which I was surprised at to be honest, but then he really was a gentleman in every sense of the word.

He poured two cut-glass tumblers of brandy and led me to the bedroom. Arvid undressed me and himself and asked me to lie still he then began slowly kissing me, first on my neck then he worked his way down my body. He took his time and it had been a long time since I could remember a man so unselfish in bed with me.

I was moaning and writhing, the feeling was incredible. Eventually, he made love to me, this was the most incredible experience, as we both arrived at ecstasy together, he held me tight.

All I could think about was I nearly missed this opportunity. He asked if we

19

could keep in touch. Too right we can I thought as I dressed that morning to get back to my hotel and meet the girls. We swapped addresses and phone numbers and he kissed me one more time before I left. I did a little sexy wave to him as I walked away. I felt like I was walking on air. Now it was time to get my head together and help Ju get her daughter back.

The hotel looked even worse in the daylight. I walked into the hotel lobby and saw Helen sitting in a red high-backed Chesterfield leather chair that really had seen better days, she was holding a white handkerchief to her mouth and was crying. "Hells bells, what's the matter"? "It's Julie"!! "Is she o.k.? Helen, tell me what's happened"?

THE STUNNER 4

She handed me a crumpled piece of paper, in poorly-written English it said "We have your friend. You need to leave Moscow or your friend will leave Moscow in a box. DO NOT GO TO THE THE LAW"

This is typical of my life, one minute up then the next down. I had to take charge, Helen was so upset, blaming us for leaving Ju, I felt we had let her down but it was no good looking for scapegoats it was Ju we had to find. "Look Helen, we have to think about this, let's find a coffee shop and think about what we can do". Zazas was a small coffee shop we found on a back street.

I had never seen Helen so distressed, I knew how bad this was then it suddenly hit me, could Nils or Arvid help us? They must know people. I rang him and told him what had happened, he said not to leave the café and he would be with us in twenty minutes.

Just to have somebody who knew the place was a relief of sorts, we waited and Helen had calmed down by the time Arvid arrived and ordered more coffee, this was going to be a long day.

"I need a full description of your friend; a picture would help as well". Helen remembered she had taken a picture of us getting on the plane. Arvid wrote everything down. "Can you help us"? "I think so, but first, we need to get you out of the hotel, you can stay at my apartment, you will be safe there".

THE STUNNER 4

Why is my life so crazy I thought as I sat with Helen in Arvid's apartment? Helen was very quiet and too upset to talk so I decided to have a look around. In the dining area were a lot of pictures of Avid in what looked like a military uniform. Beside one picture where he is being presented with a medal was a written and signed letter from the Supreme Commander of the Swedish Army and for some reason, it was written in English.

"Arvid Glick on this day was presented with the highest honour the Swedish Military can bestow, the Medal of Merit for his bravery while serving in a Special Operations Group when he single-handedly, while under enemy fire, rescued three wounded colleagues from their danger"

Just then I heard him come in. I panicked. "Oh, Arvid where is your loo"? he pointed but I wasn't convinced he didn't know I had been snooping.

"I will make us a coffee ladies then I have some news to tell you". This all sounded positive from Arvid.

Bloody hell, I was quite excited, not only was this guy a hunk and a nice guy, but he had also served in Sweden's S.A.S equivalent and I just dropped across him. Talk about somebody on your side when you need them, I was like a cat with nine lives.

Helen had calmed down quite a bit now. "Right ladies, this is the situation. Julie is alive but they are hunting you two". "Who are they"? "They call themselves

THE STUNNER 4

АД НА КОЛЕСАХ which roughly translates in English to "HELL ON WHEELS" They started out as ordinary railwaymen who would leave their families for sometimes years to earn money to feed them. They lived and worked in the harshest of conditions and realised that the Russian police and businessmen would take advantage of their families so they banded together to create this band of brothers, soon, many of the army secretly joined their ranks as they were away from home for long periods as well.

They are very well organised and are designed to protect men and their families from wrongdoings. In the case of your friend, make no mistake, if her husband gives the word she will be killed and fed to the wolves. At the moment he has chosen to take her hostage, if you leave the country, I'm pretty sure they will torture her and make her sign a legally binding document giving up any rights to the child.

There is also a fair chance all three of you would be arrested at the airport on a trumped-up charge that would never allow you to come to Russia ever again. So, you see, they have the upper hand. Tonight, we sleep, then we find your friend before it's too late. Helen this is your room. Saron, you have my room, I will sleep on the couch". Not if I had anything to do with it, I thought. I waited for Helen to go to bed then I beckoned Arvid into the bedroom, we kissed passionately and he held me tightly, my

26

heart was thumping as he caressed me. I could feel his excitement pressed against me. He picked me up, he was so strong then gently laid me on the white cotton sheets. Nothing was rushed with Arvid, he was a very sensual lover. He explored all of my body like nothing I had experienced before, his only concern was my fulfilment. We rolled and I ended on top feeling every bit of him as I writhed in pure ecstasy, hardly able to control my body from its pleasure. Eventually, it was over, the feeling I had was hard to describe. I felt warm and safe, even with what was happening. He held me for a short while but said it was best if he went back in the living room in case Helen got up, he didn't want her to think we were taking the situation lightly. I understood

but my whole body ached for him to be
next to me.

Chapter 2

The following morning, Arvid was making an English breakfast, was there any end to this man's talents? I felt so guilty telling him I would just have a poached egg on toast because I was a veggie. He said he wasn't sure but where we were going would be very cold and I needed fuel inside me so he did a big bowl of porridge with honey as well, for me of course.

Helen, the gannet on the other hand, woofed the lot down. "Mate, I don't how you keep that figure with what you can eat and drink". Helen laughed for the first time since poor Ju had been taken. "Put it down to sex, well, I can dream "she said, laughing again.

THE STUNNER 4

"Right girls, I am going to meet some blokes who I am hoping will help us". "Arvid, if they want the money that is not a problem, I just want you to know we just want Julie back safe and sound". "I will be back after lunch, don't go out and don't answer the door to anyone, are we clear on this"? Helen and I both simultaneously said yes.

He left and we sat talking. "Well, this is no cake walk Saron, I thought we would get the hassle off her husband but not some renegade gang".

"Other countries are so different to England Helen". "I'm learning that now, think I'm a bit wet behind the ears mate". "Don't worry, we will get her back" and I showed her the medal picture and the citation. "Oh, does that mean he is like that Andy McNab who was in the SAS and wrote those books on it? My nutty ex used to read them all the time".

It was almost 2.00 p.m. when Arvid returned. "I wasn't planning on taking you with us to get your friend back but these lads that are going to help said the Hell on Wheels crew would probably find you so you had best come along".

"Where is she"? "They said their contacts said she is in her grandma's house with her child. This will be very dangerous, I can get you a flight out of here through the Embassy but they can't be seen to be helping your friend, it's like poking your nose into another countries business. I think that's how you English say it".

THE STUNNER 4

It made me smile at this hunk of a Swedish body trying hard to understand English. Funnily enough, I wasn't frightened of what we were about to do, having killed before and been in the dangerous situations I had been in, it wasn't really a surprise, on the other hand, Helen needed my reassurances, she was bricking it, as we say.

Arvid's car wasn't much of a vehicle but beggars can't be chooser's, we set off with Arvid. Poor Helen was a bit on edge. The men that were going to help followed. We hadn't been introduced because what we didn't, know we couldn't tell.

I was beginning to realise just how stupid we had been to think we could go to a foreign country and pick up Julie's baby. I was starting to feel guilty about Ju and Helen but if we had any chance, it was with Arvid. I was dreamingly thinking about him when he leaned forward and that's when I noticed he had a gun in a holster across his chest. What was this guy? It did make me think that he said he had a desk job at the Embassy I don't think so.

"So, is Gustav's grandmother still living in Moscow"? I showed him the address we had. "No, they have moved to Tarlinski by the lake". We arrived and Arvid said we were about a mile away and the vehicles had to be hidden in the forest, he said it was on foot from here.

THE STUNNER 4

It was so flipping cold, the four men in the other vehicle arrived and one brushed over the tyre tracks. Surprisingly, they all spoke good English which they communicated to Arvid.

"We don't know if their friend is alone with the grandmother and the baby, our intelligence is suggesting that there is just them in the house but they have three guards and a sniper, first, we take the sniper out so Dima and Igor, you sort that then radio me and then we will take out the guards. You come back to bring my car and your van then we leave".

It all sounded well-drilled I thought. "Dima and Igor, go now". They disappeared through the deep snow and were soon out of sight. "O.k., now we wait for the call".

Arvid could see Helen was really nervous, he said she should stay in the car and, just remember he said, "Remember it's very cold, if you pee in your pants, you only stay warm for so long" I didn't know if he was serious or joking then he laughed it was his way of trying to lighten the situation for Helen.

"So, Helen, you sit tight, don't get out of the car, you will get lost out here and there are bears and wolves, you won't last five minutes".

About thirty minutes later the call came through, Igor said the sniper was no more. "O.K. we move now, Strabin, Hoxin, check your weapons, you take the two at the front door I take the back door. Saron, you stand back, on my signal you come in the house".

Everything happened so quickly and he signalled me into the cabin. Inside, we found a bruised Julie with Ezlynn and an old lady with a headscarf on and what my grandma called a pinafore, she had grey unkempt hair. She said something in Russian and Igor hit her so hard he knocked her clean off the chair. The old lady, Ezlynn and Julie all screamed.

"O.k. the vehicles are back here, she is coming with us" Arvid said, pointing to the old lady. Ju looked terrible but, in another way, relieved. She had her little girl back. Back in the forest, Arvid thanked Igor and his team then came back to us in the car, they had taken the old lady. "What happens now Arvid"?

"The only reason they would help us was because the old lady would know where Gustav was and that would lead them to the Hell on Wheels gang but enough of that, we need to get you over the border, flying is too risky".

He turned to Julie here and he gave her a passport for Ezlynn. "So, where are you taking us"? Helen enquired, having now got her mojo back.

"We have a fourteen-hour drive before we get to Poland, my friend will meet us one hour from the border and that is as far as I can take you". I felt sad, I really liked Arvid and so wanted us to keep in touch. "Are we stopping on the way"?

THE STUNNER 4

"No, we have to keep going, it is too dangerous.

I sat in the front, Helen, Julie and Ezlynn were in the back and soon asleep. I felt tired but it was only fair to keep Arvid company on such a long drive, I thought maybe the last three hours they would be awake then I could get some shut eye.

"I will never be able to thank you enough for what you have done for Helen and all of us? He smiled at me and I wanted to hug him, this is so bloody unfair I thought. "Arvid, will you keep in touch"? "Yes, of course. This is my phone number Saron" then I gave him my number.

Sure enough, one hour from the border and his friend was waiting. Arvid said the car was in my name so there should be no problem. We transferred across to the other car and we all thanked Arvid, it was a weird situation, this man, and now his friend who we didn't know, had been so kind to us, it showed human kindness is still out there in this crazy world.

He waved us off and we set off for the Polish border. It wasn't like I expected. Two official-looking guys with machine guns walked over to the car. In broken English, they said they were arresting me and that the others were to drive to their destination. At this Helen went ballistic but they weren't changing their minds and bundled me into a car leaving the others in a state of panic.

Chapter 3

Little was I to know how this incident
was going to impact my life and I guess
everybody's lives. It was almost two
hours I figured when we arrived at their
equivalent of a Police Station. They said
it was Gnarski pronounced Narski. They
took me into a dingy room, I assumed I
was in Poland, it would be a big mistake
to think that I was back in Russia.

I decided to ask for somebody to call the
Swedish Embassy and ask for Arvid. I
knew I shouldn't have, I didn't want to
get him in trouble but I was desperate.

They put me in a dingy cell and had not
charged me with anything. It felt like a
couple of hours had passed when this
scruffy looking man came to my cell and

spoke to me in broken English, which was just audible. He proceeded to tell me that the Embassy had said there was nobody there of that name.

Now I was seriously worried, what the hell was going on? A week went by before any more developments. I had shitty food. just water to drink and not enough of that. I felt lousy. there were no showers, just a cold tap in a crazed sink.

What the bloody hell was going on? They sat me in this dingy room with the two goons who had arrested me.

"So, Miss Leila was guilty I think" and he pushed two bags with white powder in them across the table to me. "Five kilos of heroin found in your bag. How do you explain that"? "What the hell are you on about? I don't have drugs, in fact I detest them, what is this all about"?

"Miss Leila, our prisons are full of innocent people" the fat ugly one laughed and drew hard on his smelly cigarette before blowing his disgusting smoke everywhere.

"So, we have drugs and that means a minimum eight-year jail sentence". "I want a lawyer". The other guy just laughed, his double chin gyrating up and down like two dolphins playing, even with all the trouble I was apparently in I still had confidence in myself.

These two goons just kept banging on about the drugs. Eventually, they took me back to another cell which I was sharing with another woman, she must have been

42

twenty stones and she just stared at me. Eventually, she spoke. You aren't going to believe this but she was Irish, in fact so Irish was her brogue I had all on understanding but the gist of it was, she said she was in for drugs as well. I tried to explain that I had been stitched up. She laughed then said something to me that sent a shiver down my spine. "You have bigger worries in here pretty girl. You have the dykes and the male prison guards to watch out for". "I don't intend to stay here long". "What, do you think you will have a trial? and she laughed showing just one bottom tooth and three top teeth. "You won't get a trial, drugs are a massive problem here, they will just lock you up". "They can't do that"! "Who are you going to complain to"?

THE STUNNER 4

"How long have you been in"? "They gave me seventeen years, I have eight left I think, time means nothing in here, one woman has been in here twenty-eight years and they said it would be three, they have just forgotten about her"!!

"That's crazy and those drugs were planted on me". I told her the story about what had happened. "Well, you must have really pissed somebody off lady. My name is Mary". "Oh, I'm Saron. Do you think my friends will be o.k."? "I am guessing so, they have you for some reason. My tip to you is to stick close to me, don't stare at anybody, that is like signing your death warrant, keep your eyes to the floor but if you do get challenged, you can't back down, here" and she gave me what looked like a sharp pin with a cloth handle.

"Carry that with you at all times and if you have to use it go here, on the jugular. Deaths are never questioned; they just take them away. I think, as far as they are concerned, it's a drug dealer less to keep".

That first night, I lay in the top bunk unable to sleep, the noise was intense, in some respects I guess I was lucky to be sharing with Mary, for one she spoke the same language and two, she knew her way around this place. I had to stay strong some months had gone by and I stuck to the rules Mary had taught me and it seemed like even the guards would wide berth me because of Mary.

THE STUNNER 4

We used to play chess, Mary taught me and sometimes, but not very often, we would get a book delivery, they were almost all Russian or Polish so not much use but the odd time we got an English or American and that felt like a treat. A treat, I mean, blood hell, some shabby book, what had my life come to?

I wondered about Helen and Ju, why had nobody come to get me? What about Arvid? I did not believe they had contacted the Swedish Consulate. I wondered if Helen or Ju had contacted them. It was during one of the very deep-thinking moments that I remembered that the solicitor from Fowey had tried to contact me a few times before we left for this ill-fated trip to Russia and wondered what he wanted?

THE STUNNER 4

I had been in this hell hole for almost a year when I was summoned to this guy's office, I suppose he was the head of the prison. He was actually quite friendly towards me and offered me a coffee and a biscuit. The biscuit was a bit like biscotti but not at all sweet.

"So, Miss Saron Leila, I have news of your sentence for drug trafficking". I remembered what Mary had said I wasn't to argue just take the punishment, that way they would let you out quicker. "The courts have decided that, due to your good behaviour, that a sentence of fourteen years be reduced to eight of which, you have served one year and two months, again, because of your acceptance of your punishment, this will also be deducted meaning you will serve six years and ten months". He waved his hand at guards gesturing to take me back to my cell. I was in shock, if I had protested it would have been fourteen years! I vowed then to find out who framed me and why!!

I was counting down the years and now that I had been here 3 years, I was praying my good behaviour might see my sentence cut again.

It was a usual day that saw me and Mary playing chess, I thought I was going to be Grandmaster by the time I leave. "Saron, you have a visitor". My heart raced, had my friends found me or maybe Arvid? "Hurry, follow me".

He took me along the dingy corridor into a room where a guy with jet black greased hair and sunglasses was sitting. I was instructed to sit across from this man.

"Who are you, what do you want?" "Saron, you don't remember me. I am" and he took his glasses off. I was speechless. "Prison is nice, yes"? "No, it's bloody awful". "So, you have about just short of four years before you could be released". "Yes, but why are you bothered"? "After what you did to my mother Angelique, I'm not bothered at all but I have a proposition for you. You stole my inheritance, I am Luca Ricci's son, Michael, and vengeance will be mine".

"What the hell are you talking about"? "All of your inheritance you will sign away or I will ensure you never leave this prison. If you don't, believe me, I will prove to you, the idiot you share a cell with is due an early release, just so you know, she will be involved in a scuffle and a weapon will be found on her and she will have another ten years added to her sentence. So, while we have been having a nice little talk the scuffle already happened so there is nothing you can do about it.

I will return in the next week with the paperwork, goodbye until next week Saron". The guards grabbed me by my arm but shook hands with Michael. It suddenly hit me, he had set me up and he wanted my fortune. and it wasn't looking like my choices were that good if I wanted to get out of here. Back at my cell, Mary was being moved out, I tried to talk to her but she was in a dark place and the guards pushed me back into my cell. One of them said, "In one week, you will want to sign up for Mr Michael, if you don't, your replacement cellmate will make your life hell". He laughed and said something to the other guard about being rich soon.

Bloody Michael had cut deals with everybody. The only thing on my mind was revenge, but first, I had to get out of this hell hole.

The day had come and the same guard came. "If you don't sign and you don't any longer have fat Mary, I will get something out of this, we will take you every day". This made my mind up. No way was this going to happen.

Just one thing was bothering me, if he was Angelique's son, he wouldn't be this guy's age so who was he? This I was saving until I got out.

Michael, as he called himself, sat across from me with some paperwork which he took out of his crocodile skin briefcase. "Before I sign anything, I want some guarantees". "Oh, you think you are calling the shots pretty lady, so what might they be".

"First, I sign this and you give me five hundred dollars and I leave today", with a snap of his fingers the guard brought my clothes and the Canada Goose jacket I had on when they arrested me and placed them on the table.

THE STUNNER 4

Michael also gave me a train ticket from Russia to Poland, then onto France and a ferry ticket to Dover. "I am a man of my word, this is business Saron and, besides. you bought them" and he laughed.

"O.K., but how was this set up"? "Well, firstly, Gustav is part of the team and we needed to get you here so he took the little girl. That's where Arvid came in, he doesn't work for the Swedish Consulate and we knew you would look around his apartment so we setup the pictures of him with a Medal of Merit" at this the prat laughed. "It went so well, everything ran like clockwork". "So, who were the Hell on Wheels and the men who helped us get Ezlynn and Julie"? "They all worked for us". "But they shot people"? "All fake my dear, all fake". "So why has it taken so long to get to this point"? "Well, first of all, a bit of revenge for Angelique and other people who you pissed off. Our solicitors are in contact with your solicitors so as soon as you sign, a motorbike courier will take the signed documents and by the time you get to France, you will be plain old Saron Leila, oh, and by the way, you will need to find somewhere to live because your house, the cottage in Polruan, will be sold".

I looked through the paperwork, the diamond mines, all my accounts and personal wealth is to be signed away. I didn't see mine and Ju's café so maybe they couldn't touch that because it was shared and I think it had Ju as the leading name on the business registry.

THE STUNNER 4

My choices were nil so I signed, he then handed me my clothes and five hundred pounds, he laughed and said he couldn't give me the other five hundred because it was greedy of me. You have to admire his cheek having just taken everything I owned off me. He clearly didn't know Saron I thought. We crossed the border, money changed hands, then he had told me the same would happen in France and after that, I was on my own. As I got on the train in Poland, I remember thinking my life was going to be so different, I was just hoping Ju had kept the café going, at least I had somewhere to live and work.

THE STUNNER 4

Chapter 4

From Poland to Paris then the Eurostar to St Pancras, London, the guy taking me was quite nice, he somehow didn't fit with the rest of them. He started to tell me how they knew I had killed the main guys but they didn't know how so they hatched a plan.

"They found out that Gustav was having an affair and warned him they would inform his wife. They subtly suggested that Ezlynn would be taken off him knowing he would run for Russia, exactly where they wanted you, then part two, Arvid was chosen to be the good Samaritan and you fell for it. Nobody died that day but they had you.

THE STUNNER 4

The intention was to keep you in prison for seven years but they wanted their money so, over three years was considered a fair rate for your misdemeanours"!!

I sat open-mouthed listening to how I was set up. He asked if I wanted a coffee so, I said yes because I assumed he would leave his coat, sure enough, he did so I went through his pockets, he was only bloody Russian police so obviously on the take. I decided to put on my womanly charms. His name was Ali Kasandai.

"You are so nice" I said, crossing my legs to get his interest. "I wish I could see you again". "That would be dangerous Saron, for me, you must never repeat what I just told you". "Of course not, why don't you wait until I have settled in the U.K. then come over for a couple of weeks? Nobody needs to know, it's my way of saying thank you". "Let me think about it. This is my email address" and he wrote it down. I knew then I had him hooked. He put me on the shuttle from Paris to my final destination back to London, I kissed him seductively, I had to put everything into this because I was going to need him if the plan I was working out in my head was going to work.

He waved me off and I eventually arrived at St Pancras and booked into a Holiday Inn by the station, I felt drained. I checked in and got to my room. I dropped my bag and flopped on the bed and that was when the emotion hit me.

THE STUNNER 4

I cried and cried, I just couldn't stop, the reality had hit home, I'd had everything but now nothing. I looked in the mirror. Come on Saron, get a grip I thought. The following morning, I got the train to Cornwall.

My heart was pounding as I walked down the steps to the Bistro Café, I could see two people sitting having a drink, I was pretty sure it was two women so I tapped on the sliding doors, I could then see Helen coming towards me and she let out the biggest scream.

"Saron? But you are dead". "What"? "They told us you were shot trying to escape". Julie realised it was me and ran over crying, we were all hugging, it was incredibly emotional.

I sat down with them and told them the whole story. They sat opened mouthed, "So they have taken everything"? "Yes, everything, I have nothing, other than a half share in this".

I could see my words made both Julie and Helen feel uncomfortable. "What is it, girls"?

"Well, when we got back here, Helen decided to stay and help me with this place, I decided that Ezlynn would live with mum and dad they had bought a static caravan and moved down here so I get to see her but if Gustav comes looking, he won't find her. After eighteen months we were told you had tried to escape and had been shot. When we left, Arvid said we must never return but he would work at getting you out so you can imagine our shock and horror when Arvid called to say you were dead but he said he would sort your funeral. We never heard anymore. It was a hard few months, after all that and eventually I asked Helen to share the place with me".

My heart sank. I could tell Helen felt bad, "It's your share mate and you are back and alive, it's only fair you take it back". "Helen, that is so kind, look, why don't we split it three ways"? They were both relieved. "Great, let's go to the solicitor tomorrow and sort the paperwork. Helen, get some Prosecco and we were going to have one of our drunken nights". While Helen was sorting the drink, Julie said, "The solicitor had tried to contact you quite a few times but, when we sorted this place, because we thought you were dead, he told us that he had been asked for paperwork about your properties etc but he didn't wasn't to hand them over unless you were ok with it". "Do you know if he did"? "I don't know". "He must have Ju, let's see what he has to say tomorrow". Luckily, the Café Bistro was shut at this time of year and now with me taking one of the apartments, there were no letting apartments left so we weren't sure how this would affect the business. It felt good to be with my mates again and you know what, yes, I loved being rich but friendship is worth more. I did worry about the islanders but they were set up so the people who took my wealth shouldn't be able to touch theirs, thank goodness.

THE STUNNER 4

We were drinking until 3.00 a.m. and it hit that me I was out of practise Ju was dancing to Roxy music. Helen, the bloody beer monster, was pouring us all the last bottle which was number six. She gave me my drink then put her arms around me and hugged me. "I am so happy tonight that you aren't dead and are with me and Julie". "I'm sort of glad I'm not dead too Hells"! and we both laughed. Ju was in her own world. probably dancing with Bryan Ferry in her mind.

We all staggered to bed, luckily, we had decided to go to the solicitors after lunch The only boat across to Fowey was on the hour because it was the closed season. Helen looked green as we crossed the Estuary, I wasn't looking forward to seeing the solicitor, I was convinced he was crooked from way back when he was dealing with Luca so we didn't particularly like each other.

It was a shock when we got there and they said my solicitor had sold up and retired but Mr Cain would look after my account if I so wished. Even that sounded dodgy to me, I bet he was paid off I thought. We went through the three-way split and it was obvious this guy knew nothing about me, maybe that was a good thing.

I felt pleased I had such good friends, I decided I was going to get my revenge and I know you must think I'm nuts, why not just settle down and serve cream teas and afternoon teas? Well, I'm sorry but when I started on this road, I was going to say adventure but you would have to be psychotic to think this has been an adventure. One thing was for certain, I can't let them do to me what they did and I will seek out each one and pay them back.

Back in my apartment, I started drafting a list of people who required payback. I then spent weeks researching poison although the best way would be how I had done it before.

For any of this to work, I had to build up the trust with Ali Kasandi. There were still eight weeks before the season started so I had a fair bit of time on my hands which I knew would not be available to me after that.

THE STUNNER 4

First of all, I had to stockpile the poison I was going to need. By week three, I had enough hidden in the apartment, it was over breakfast with Ju one morning when she suddenly said, "You want revenge, don't you"? "Julie, they took everything I worked so hard for and nearly lost you in the process so, yes, I do".

"Go on then, what's your plan"? "The guy I told you about, Ali Kasandi, I will seduce him, get all the names of the people who did this to me and boy will I then have a list". "But Saron, that would mean you going to Russia again and they won't let you in will they"? "I will get a different passport and change my appearance". "You really are going to do this, aren't you"? "Ju, you have known me long enough to know I never give in to anyone". Julie rolled her eyes and put the breakfast dishes in the sink.

"Well, tell you what, lets me, you and Helen go into St Ives, get a taxi in and hit the bars". "I'm up for that. Where is Helen"? "You know she likes her bed, I'll give her a shout and tell her what we are doing".

I know it was St Ives and not St Tropez but its needs must at the minute, I had my brown skin-tight leather Alexander McQueen trousers on with a brilliant white, equally skin-tight blouse tied at the waist to show my diamond belly piercing. I wore a black bra under it, I had seen some big movie star in the same outfit and she really did look sexy and that's how I felt, it was the pickup I needed.

THE STUNNER 4

"Bloody hell Saron, with those shoes on, can you walk"? Helen was referring to my Christian La Boutin brown shoes with six-inch heels. "Well, I can walk now but I'm not sure about at the end of the day Helen"! and Julie laughed.

The taxi dropped us at the first pub on beer quest, The Castle Inn. It was now 1.30 p.m. so a bit early for the locals and the pubs we were hitting first were more local pubs, the plan was to hit the more tourist frequented pubs after 7.00 p.m. to see if, as Helen put it, if there was any gorgeous talent out. "Yes, ladies, what can I get you"? "Three double Hendricks with a splash of tonic in each one please". The young girl duly obliged and we sat on the bar stools.

"Cheers, girls and thanks for everything". "You would have done much more for me and Julie Saron". "The three degrees" Helen said, "Bottoms up" and she downed hers like it was a glass of water. I managed to down mine and eventually Ju did the same. "Right, come on, next one on the list". "There is the Cabbage, just up the road" the young girl said. "Thank you, sweetheart" and we turned left out of the doors and up about a hundred yards to the Cabbage, it was a bit grotty, there were all the out of work boys in there and a few old soaks. You can imagine what looks we got walking in, there were a few wolf whistles. The lad behind the bar asked if we were lost. "Cheeky buggar" Helen said. "Three gins with tonic clever buggar" she said, the young lad coloured up. "It will have to be house gin, do you want doubles for an extra fifty pence"? Asking Helen that was like asking somebody who hadn't eaten for a week if they wanted a slap-up meal. "Of course,", she replied then turned to us "Stupid boy" she said.

We didn't stop long, the gin was like drinking grease and even beer monster Helen struggled with hers.

"Next bar then girls. The last one up here is the Soldier Dick". We walked a few hundred yards and the pub was on the corner. "This is more like it, puts some tunes on Ju while I get the drinks". "It's my turn Saron"". "Don't worry Ju, I'll get the drinks while you and Helen pick the tunes".

THE STUNNER 4

I could feel myself getting a buzz as I ordered the next drinks. My little booty was up for a dance. Ju had put on Uptown girl and I felt great as I walked with the drinks towards the little dance floor, I could feel the eyes of the pub on me and I felt like Christie Brinkley in the video, confidently striding out.

Saron is back I thought. I felt so sexy in my skin-tight brown leather trousers. Straight after that song, Helen had chosen Out on the floor by Dobie Gray. I was swallowed up in a world of my own as I used all the dance floor.

We had two drinks there then the beer monster that Helen was said, "Come on girls, time to hit the town"! As I walked out, I passed this guy and I could have

sworn it was Adam out of Coronation
Street, I had seen he was clocking me
earlier on. He was well dressed and
winked at me as I went past. "Maybe see
you later" he said. I just smiled, well a
girl can't be too keen to show hey?

"Right, The Sloop next", "Whoop" Helen
shouted. "You o.k. Ju"? "Just worried
about you and what you said you were
going to do. I don't want to lose my mate
again". "You won't Ju, trust me on this,
now come, on its boogie time"!

The Sloop was in full voice, it had always
been one of the most popular pubs in
Cornwall with locals and a few tourists
who seemed to come down even before
the season started.

THE STUNNER 4

"Here you go girl, three Sex on the Beach cocktails". "Bloody hope so Helen"! and I laughed. "Don't think you will have much trouble, did you see that guy in the other pub? He was really watching you". Some guy started chatting up Ju, well they would, she had that something guys liked.

"Hey, Saron, remember that night you stayed at mine, you had come down from Heathcliff and we had been to The Man that Winks, remember"? "Oh yeah, you copped for Gary the DJ and left me with his sidekick, bloody hell, his breath stank, think that's what made me throw up in your dads car Helen. He wasn't very chuffed was he"? "Oh, he banged on about it for years". We were rolling, I thought Ju was going to wet herself she laughed that much.

"Right next one Ju". "What about the Tin Miners"? "O.k. dokey. Come on sexy Saron". Helen by now was on a roll, poor Ju was fluffing and I was just about holding my own.

By now the pubs were getting busy and three girls who are pretty fresh and out for some fun, were attracting attention which was quite intense with both the local guys and one or two holidaymakers.

This one guy was particularly persistent with Helen. "He really is pissing me off Saron, shall we move"? "Let's finish these drinks". "I've finished mine so I'll nip to the toilet while you finish yours".

THE STUNNER 4

We watched Helen wander off and I noticed she said something to the prat.

She came back. "You o.k. mate"? "He won't take no for an answer". "Come on, let's go to the Sea Shell, they have a disco downstairs and I could do with dancing some of this alcohol off".

As we walked out, I stood on the prat's foot with my stiletto spike heel, he did just squeal. We laughed all the way to the next pub with Ju telling Helen she knew I would do something. Ju got the drinks and we got a table downstairs where the guy from one of the other pubs, remember the one I said looked like Adam Barlow? came over to our table and just sat down next to me. He turned to Helen and Ju who had just arrived back with the drinks. "Excuse me ladies but I have met the girl of my dreams". "I wish I had a hundred pounds for every man that had said things like this" I said!!

"Let me introduce myself, my name is Gary Williams". "Come on Ju, I think we are gooseberries, let's have a dance". "Oh, thanks, girls". Julie and Helen left me with Gary and headed to the dance floor to Le Chic.

"Well, I'd best stay and keep you company". I laughed, he was a right smoothie. "So, Gary, what are you doing in Cornwall"? "I'm a barrister and my case has been adjourned for two weeks in Exeter so I thought I would come down and have a few days. So glad I did, I mean, how many guys are spending the night with Cameron Diaz"? "Oh, give over". "You are surely not telling me nobody has ever said about the resemblances"? "Well yes, they have it just gets a bit old, but thank you".

"Would you like to dance to this"? "What, flipping YMCA, are you having laugh"? "Come on, I'll show you my moves" and he grabbed my arm, we passed Helen and Julie, both laughing at me going to dance to YMCA.

He was really funny on the dance floor doing all the moves, you would never have known he was a barrister and he was very good looking. Not that I was interested of course. No, behave you lot reading this, behave!

THE STUNNER 4

We had a couple more dances, he was making me laugh so much. "Let's sit down with the girls now". By now, poor Ju had wobble gob, she had all on getting her words out, that was really making Gary laugh. Helen said the taxi was here and was I going back with them.

"Yeah, see you Gary, hope your case goes well". "Can't we see each other again"? "Yeah, go on Saron", Helen said, up to her usual mischief.

"O.k. when"? "What about tomorrow. Where shall I pick you up from"? "It's a Bistro bar called "Shed of dreams" in Porthcurno". "O.K., shall we say 8.00 p.m. tomorrow night then"?

"Great, look, I'd best go, my friends are waiting". Gary leaned forward to kiss me but I slightly pulled away. I didn't know why I had agreed to another meeting, anyway, that's me int'it?

The girls were full of it when I got in the taxi, well, Helen was, Ju was at that stage of the evening where you will sleep anywhere as long as you can sleep.

We paid the taxi driver and thanked him, Ju went to bed but of course beer monster Helen wanted another drink so we cracked open the brandy.

"Can I say something Saron"? "Of course, we are best mates, aren't we"? "Yeah, but really it's none of my business". "Don't worry, ask me anything". "O.k. well, both me and Ju are worried about you with this revenge thing. Money isn't everything Saron and we all have a nice life here, why would you risk that"?

"It actually isn't about the money, although I don't intend to be poor when I'm finished but, the way I was treated and lied to needs to be paid for by the people who did this". "Well, just please be careful mate and if you need help you only have to ask, you know that don't you"? "I know, but this is my fight Helen but it's good to know you and Ju have my back, cheers" and I raised my glass of brandy.

The following day it felt like a hundred JCB's were digging in my head. Flipping Helen was fresh as a daisy but Ju was about like me. "Wish I had your constitution, Helen". "You two are light weights" and she laughed, turning over the bacon on the grill for her sandwich. The smell of it was making me heave.

Ju made me a slice of toast and she had the same, we sat like a pair of spaced-out morons trying to eat a simple slice of toast. Eventually, I told Helen and Julie I was going back to bed. Julie wasn't far behind while the beer monster munched her way through half a pig slapped between two doorstep slices of bread.

I must have been rough, Ju came into my room with a cup of tea. "What time is it mate"? "Almost 5.30 p.m. thought I'd best wake you". "Really? Blimey, I must have needed that". "I slept until 2.00 p.m. Helen has gone food shopping.

THE STUNNER 4

You are seeing that Gary at 8.00 p.m. don't forget". "Oh crap, I really don't feel like that tonight". "It will do you good, he seems like a nice guy". "I know but I'm not bothered about a boyfriend, I have too many complications in my life just now". "Just go out and enjoy it stop thinking so deep Saron. Anyway, it might take your mind off what you are thinking of doing".

I decided Ju was probably right so I put my favourite off the shoulder green Alexander McQueen dress on with some brown Gucci shoes and felt good as I climbed into Gary's silver XJS. "Where are we going"? "I have a table booked at my hotel if that is o.k."? "Where are you staying"? "At the Coastal Grand in Port Isaac, the food looked really good, is that o.k."? "As long as they have veggies stuff then it will be fine". "Oh, crap, I didn't check". "Don't worry, most places do now".

We arrived and this place was sumptuous, it was modelled on a French Chateau, there were massive chandeliers everywhere and a waiter showed us to our table. It was all very romantic but to be honest it was a bit over the top for a first date, this guy was flash or really trying to impress. Gary ordered champagne, I guess trying to impress me, if only he knew I used to drink the best Champagne back in the day.

Anyway, he seemed quite nice, a bit pompous perhaps. He told me he was a barrister and grew up in Aiwick but moved when he was qualified and set his practice up in Staffordshire in Uttoxeter would you believe it!!

At the end of the night, he dropped me off, kissed me on the cheek then asked if I would go to Staffordshire for a long weekend. I said I would think about it and call him. To be honest, I quite fancied going back home.

The following day the girls were giving me the twenty-question game. I was honest, he didn't really float my boat but my life didn't seem to have many happy options at the moment so I rang Gary and said I would see him next Saturday and asked him to send me the address. I hadn't said I was from Leek, I wanted to know more about him first.

THE STUNNER 4

We had started preparing the Café Bistro ready for opening day. Friday came around and I left the girls to it, the address Gary gave I knew, it was a small village called Grindon near Butterton. He said his cottage was about a hundred yards from the pub called The Cavalier.

Chapter 5

It was a good six-hour drive and I got to the cottage, aptly called Moonlight View, Daffodil Hill. I must admit I was a bit nervous, I mean, I hardly knew the guy. I walked up the neat little cottage garden path and Gary must have heard me pull up, he opened the door. "Hey, I wasn't sure you would come". "Why"? "I didn't get the impression you were over impressed in Cornwall". "Sorry, I just had a lot on my mind, nothing against you".

His cottage was neat but not homely and didn't appear very lived in so I questioned my thoughts with him. "Well, to be honest, I was in a relationship until about eight months ago and we split so she took most of the stuff. My job takes me to several cities, you know London, Newcastle, Liverpool etc. So, I spend a fair time in hotel rooms so don't get a chance to put my own mark on the place. Look, freshen up and if you want and we can walk to the Cavalier and have an evening meal". "O.k., that would be nice". I changed into a little mini skirt and wore a crisp white blouse and some calf-length black boots. It was a lovely night as we crossed a small stream and headed down to the pub. The Cavalier was a small, double fronted stone building, over the door carved into the stone it said, "For King and Country 1641". "Wow, this place must be old Gary". "It was a lot bigger but in 1649 Cromwell's army came through and stayed the night, all was good until they were leaving and one of them noticed that carved stone. They dragged the innkeeper and his wife out and took them to the little ford we crossed where they cut their throats, the ford ran red with blood and the locals to this day call it Blood Ford, they then ransacked the pub and set fire to it. Luckily it was a stormy night so the main building didn't get damaged while the locals fought frantically with the fire".

"That's really interesting, did you research it"? "No, Morris who sits at the bar is a local historian and anybody new to the village he tells them the story. We can have a walk around the village tomorrow, it's quite interesting". "Sounds great".

THE STUNNER 4

Gary ordered the fish pie and Saron had the Californian salad. "This is very nice Gary". "Yes, it has a good reputation for food, as you can see, it's busy for a little pub Saron". Gary seemed a nice guy but something was nagging at me about him which I couldn't put my finger on. Maybe it was just me not wanting a relationship, I mean, he wasn't bad looking or anything. I know what you lot are thinking, to go for it girl.

"So, Saron, you said you help run that Bistro Café in Cornwall. What led you to that career? I would have thought with your looks and figure you must have done modelling, are you from Cornwall? Your accent is very much like Staffordshire". "I lived everywhere during my teenage years we were in

Yorkshire. Julie and Helen are my best friends so we like working together".

"If you don't mind me saying, the Bistro must be very successful, you wear some really expensive clothes and shoes". "It does o.k. Gary, anyway, you being a barrister, you lot charge the earth"! Gary laughed. "Come on, let's have a dessert". I felt a bit decadent so went for the Le Fleur de Chocolat which was a marshmallow tea cake with mint pieces which was somewhat of a surprise. Gary had the same. "Why is it in French"? "The owner's wife is French and it's her little indulgence".

"Gary, I have had a lovely evening but the drive up here took it out of me, do you mind if we go back"? "Not a problem" and we walked back. I knew there was no way I was sleeping with him, in fact, I thought about getting Ju to call me and say they had a problem and could I get back. It's awful when you have to hurt somebody's feelings, I have never been any good at that. I lay on my bed, I think Gary was a bit done but the driving excuse held him at bay at least for now.

I decided to do the walk in the morning then make out I had to go back. We were both up bright and early and I fancied a coffee so Gary said why don't we walk to Wetton Mill have a bacon sandwich and a coffee. He said he hadn't had a chance to go shopping. Again, something was telling me things were not what they seemed. Anyway, we landed at a lovely old mill by the stream and had bacon sandwiches, we each then took what was left of our coffees with us.

We climbed back up the steep hill until we came across a barn, on the side was one of the information posters, it was showing you a walk, it said that during the civil war that actual barn was used as a makeshift hospital for Royalists when they lost a battle to Cromwell's army on that very field!!

We carried on up to the little church and sat on one of the benches. Julie could not have timed calling me any better. "Excuse me" and I stood up to take call, she was in a bit of a panic, the guy who had been the chef had called her to say he wasn't coming back for another season, apparently, he had got back with the mother of his child in Newcastle and they were going to try and make a go of it.

I told her I would come back, of course Ju said they were fine and I just said I will explain later. Gary asked if I had to go back? "Yes, I'm so sorry." "That's a big shame, I know it's early days in our relationship but I have been researching my family tree and it appears that my great grandmother is buried in Moscow and I was going to ask if you would like to come with me for a few weeks before your season starts and my next case is in four weeks". Bloody hell I thought, Bingo, I could get there and lose this guy, go and do what I had to do and never see him again.

THE STUNNER 4

"Oh, that sounds great, when are you going"? "It would have to be this Thursday". "You know what," I said, all confidently, "I'll come with you, book the tickets and give me a ring, you have really excited me, thank you". I think Gary thought he had cracked it, little did he know my plan.

I drove back down to Cornwall wondering what Ju and Helen would say. Yes, I'm headstrong but I have to do this so I decided to tell them both the day before I was to meet Gary.

I had to work out how to get the poison over to Russia, I had decided to place it in a makeup bag and ask Gary to take it in his carryon luggage, that way, if they stop him, I will deny I even know the bloke.

THE STUNNER 4

Back in Cornwall, the girls were chuffed to see me and wanted to know if I had met the love of my life. Hardly I thought. I didn't mention Thursday yet but beavered away in my apartment making a list of the people I was determined to murder.

Wednesday night soon came around and so it was time, I told them. Helen begged me not to do it, even saying she would follow me. Ju on the other hand was subdued, she knew that her ex-husband was on my list I guessed.

"I do realise how dangerous this is girls but they took everything, they abused me and I lived in hell in Russia and they have to pay". Helen and Ju knew I was strong-willed so wished me all the best,

THE STUNNER 4

The following morning, Gary phoned, he said the Russian Airline company said there had been a delay with the flight, he said he had set off and did I want to meet him at Watford Gap services, he said a friend had a nice restaurant in Fidgety Fog, a small village near there and he hadn't seen Franco, the owner for a couple of years. Why not, I said, I had loaded the car anyway. I reckoned I would be there for around 1.30 p.m. and told him I was driving a Green Mini but would call when I parked up.

I didn't particularly mind driving but with so much to think about today, it seemed to be a pain.

I was spot on with the timing and pulled into the Services at 1.33 p.m. I phoned

Gary and then spotted him waving to me from his Burgundy Freelander, I locked the Mini up and headed across to him. Bloody hell, his dress sense left a lot to be desired, he had on a pair of, what looked like, golfing trousers with a polo neck shirt under a V neck jumper which was a loud orange colour. Embarrassment was an understatement as he kissed me on the cheek and helped me into the Freelander.

"How far to your friend's restaurant Gary"? He looked at me like a love-smitten puppy dog. "Fifteen minutes, tops. Are you hungry"? "Yes, I am a little". "Good, the food is excellent". I didn't particularly take much notice of where we were but we passed a village green before pulling up outside what appeared to be the restaurant which looked like it had been a shop in its former life.

His friend greeted us and Gary introduced me. "Oh, the lovely Saron, Gary has told me much about you". I thought, I hardly know this guy and I think he is under some illusion I am his bloody girlfriend. No way is that going to be a reality. It was only a small restaurant and it had a lot of pictures of Russia. "So, is this a Russian restaurant"? "You got it". "Wow, that is really unusual for the U.K. Gary". "Yes, I think he can only serve about thirty but a lot of Russians come out of London to eat here at the weekend".

"Good idea I suppose". I ordered a meatless Schi, I'd had that before but I didn't let on. "Oh, I think you will enjoy that, a friend of mine always has that". Gary ordered something in Russian, I think he was trying to impress me.

I hadn't realised the plane delay was just so he could get to his friends then say that we had best stop the night, hoping he was sleeping with me, well, guess what? He didn't have a cat in hells chance, I can assure you. Saron is not for turning, Gary had one use and that was to get me into Russia, then I can do what I set out to do

We had a nice meal and of course, he then came out with "I guess we'd best stay the night". "Only if they have a room for me Gary, I'm not like that". I think my abruptness set him back and, to be honest, he seemed a little annoyed. To be fair I had played him a bit.

That night, my bedroom door was locked and I just hoped he hadn't gone into my make-up case. The following morning, we thanked his friend and we headed to Heathrow for the flight.

We booked in and I let Gary go through security first then I went to go through, the guy looked at my passport then called another guy over, I knew something was wrong. Come with me please as I saw Gary disappear at the other side of the security.

Now it was interrogation time, they knew everything, I just said I loved Russia but it was no good, they wouldn't let me fly but they did let me go and they did

100

retrieve my case. That's it I thought. Not quite as you will see. I eventually arrived back in Cornwall and walked through the kitchen, Julie turned around and almost fainted. "Saron, you are safe"! "Of course, I am". "It's just been on the news, your flight to Russia was brought down two hours into the flight, they believed it to be a terrorist attack". "What, the plane was blown up"? "Yes". "Were there any survivors"? "Apparently not". "Sit down and I'll tell you what happened.

I explained to Julie what happened at the airport. "You are so lucky Saron". "I suppose I am but I wonder if they blew it up thinking I was on board"? "No, don't be thinking like that, let it go and let's concentrate on the business. What are we going to do about a chef at this late stage before the season"?

I'll get on to the agency in the morning and start interviewing. If we can get one, are you and Helen going to have a few days away before the season starts"? "That's a great idea mate. Right, you sort the chef and I will look at some four-day breaks". "Sounds like a plan to me. Saron, I am so glad you didn't get on that plane. Are you upset about Gary"? "Sadly, no, I had no intention of being with him". I know that sounds dreadful but this thing inside me, I just wanted revenge.

That night in bed I began to consider it, maybe the plane was brought down because of me and, who was Gary

THE STUNNER 4

Williams? I couldn't sleep so I looked him up, he said he was a Barrister. I looked up practising barristers in London, there was nothing. I spent three hours then it suddenly dawned on me, I had a picture of his car and the number plate. I then started trying to find where it was registered. That also drew a blank, it was a hire car. All I had left was to search for the house he lived in at Grindon. I remembered the name, Moonlight View, on Daffodil Hill. I looked it up and thought, this can't be correct, the house was registered to Amy and Morris Speke. Now I am confused!! By now I was getting sleepy so decided to follow it up the next day.

The following day I chased the agency and they said they had two chefs on their books, a Rod Lewington and William Mouse, that really made me laugh. I arranged to see Rod at 11.00 a.m. and then William Mouse at 2 .00 p.m.

Mr Lewington was a man in his mid-fifties I thought with a full grey beard and not particularly smart. "So, Mr Lewington, tell me a bit about your career, where you have worked etc". "Well, I was Head Chef at Miriam Bistro in the Isle of Man". "How long were you there"? "Just the one season". "O.K., when was that"? "It would have been, let me see, oh yeah, 2011". "Then where did you work"? "I took three years off". "Three years, what to do"? "Well, I lost my wife so, to be honest, I hit the bottle quite hard, I mean, I am being honest with you. Now I only have a drink socially". "O.K., so, 2014, where did you work then"? "I was in the works canteen at the steelworks in Port Talbot, Wales". "O.k. and how long were you there"? "A long time, it must have been at least eighteen months". "O.k., then what"? "Well, I decided to retrain to be a plasterer which was a three-year Government course". "I assume you passed that o.k."? "Well, to be honest, I failed my last year so started drinking again". "Have you had another job since"? "No, that's why I am being honest with you, I am hoping you'll give me a chance, I won't let you down".

I couldn't wait for the interview to end. I thanked him and said I would be in touch. I waited for the next one to come, Mr Mouse, I just know you are laughing at me saying his name. Mr Mouse arrived, he looked about thirty perhaps, he appeared a bit hippy looking, Rastafarian hair in a ponytail, on his wrists were leather-like bracelets. Never judge a book by its cover my dad always said. "So, is it ok to call you William"? "All my friends call me Mickey". I almost wet myself. "You are kidding, right"? "No, right from starting school they called me Mickey so I'm used to it, to be honest".

At least this one had a sense of humour. "So, where have you worked"? "I worked under Graham Plant, the T.V. chef for four years, then I went to work for Franco Marinello in Italy for two years, then I was the second chef at Stefan Hummel's restaurant in Mayfair". "Wow, do you have any recommendations on you"?

"Yes" and he pulled out a letter from these famous chefs. "So where are you now"? "Well, I left Mr Hummel's place to move to Cornwall, I love surfing you see and my girl lives down here".

"Your letters are very impressive, give me one of your signature dishes". "I do a rump steak cut into strips then marinated in Pernod overnight, then it's cooked with onions, peppers and sweet baby carrots in a cream sauce with a dash of Henderson's Relish". "Sounds lovely". "Just a minute, my signature sweet dish is pureed apricot mixed with pineapple chunks whipped cream baked on a sponge base with hint of mint". "Well Donald" and Saron laughed, "I'm so sorry, it's just". "I know, Mickey Mouse, it makes everybody laugh".

THE STUNNER 4

"Well Mickey, I am impressed, we open in three weeks and I would like you to join the team and to take our place to another level".

"Thank you Saron, that's great, you won't be disappointed". "I'm sure we won't". When he left Julie came in. "Bloody hell, I think we have snared a gem there". "Brilliant, so where do you fancy, Dublin, Benidorm or London"? "Any mate, what does Helen think"? "Benidorm". "Should have guessed that, the beer monster" and they both laughed. "Book it then Ju". "So, shall we do five days"? "Yes, I'm up for that, when"? "It will be from Monday to Friday". "That's great, I have something on this weekend". "Oh, is it a date Saron"? "I wish Helen, no, I want to find out about Gary". "You

mean Gary who was blown up"?
"Helen"! Julie said, "That's a bit harsh".
"Look you two, I am convinced that
plane was blown up expecting me to be
on it. I have to find out".

"Just be careful" they both said. "I will,
I'm leaving Friday and will be back
Sunday afternoon".

Friday came around and Saron headed for
Grindon, determined to find the truth. It
was almost 7.00 p.m. when she arrived,
having previously booked a room at the
Cavalier in Grindon. She only had an
overnight bag with her, she could hear
talking from a side room which was the
Tap Room, as they used to say. Well,
Saron being Saron did cause a stir in her

tight leather trousers white shirt and cropped leather jacket.

The young lad behind the bar couldn't stop staring at her. "Good evening" she said, parting the men standing at the bar. "I have a room booked for the night. I booked it under the name of Saron". "What a lovely name" the young lad said. "Steady on Mittens, that's a proper woman you are talking to" one of the bar huggers said.

The young lad coloured up. "Mittens, that's an unusual name". "Aye, we call him Mittens because he never takes his hands out of his pockets long enough to buy a drink so we reckon he must have cold hands and wears mittens". Saron laughed and the young lad, who by now was bright red, looked nervously at her.

"I have a room booked for the night, Saron Leila". "Oh yes, room number three, top of the stairs and first left". He handed me the key which had a big wooden ball attached to it. They must have had a few guests lose keys to have that thing stuck on the fob.

The room was surprisingly quite good. It was en-suite with a four-poster bed, lovely white cotton, Egyptian sheets and a nice array of coffee, tea and biscuits. I decided to waste no time so changed into a low-cut top, I had to sweet talk the locals if I was going to find anything out.

I strode into the bar and ordered a Hendricks gin with tonic and a slice of cucumber. "I'm Matty Treadwell" a guy said, stood next to me at the bar. "Are you on holiday"? "Just passing through" and I seized my opportunity. "Well, I was hoping to see a guy who left his coat in my Bistro in Cornwall and I was passing through from Yorkshire so thought I would drop it off for him". "What was his name"? "I only knew him as Gary but he said he lived here in Moonlight View, Daffodil Hill and it sounded idyllic so I remembered it. He said he was a Barrister". "That cottage you are on about, my missus cleans it once a week, they let it out as a holiday cottage, Major Simpson from Hartington owns the place". "Oh, do you have an address for them"?

"Yes, they live at Toad Hall, near the YHA place". "Oh, I will nip there tomorrow, they may have a forwarding address, thank you Matty". I could feel the whole pub looking at me.

I actually had a nice night, they were all nice people, buying me drinks and telling me stories. By the time my head hit the pillow, I was wasted. The following morning, I had a lovely Staffordshire breakfast then paid my bill and headed for Toad Hall in Hartington.

I was a bit shocked, I was expecting a big stately hall and Toad Hall looked like three terraced houses knocked into one.

I walked down the path with the neatly laid out borders on each side and knocked on the door.

THE STUNNER 4

A gentleman who looked in his late seventies answered the door, he had grey thinning hair and wore a tweed jacket with a yellow waistcoat, it looked like he was a clone for Rupert the Bear. "Can I help you my dear"? he said, in a plummy officious tone. "Oh, yes, sorry, my name is Saron Leila and I believe you have a cottage that you rent out in Grindon"? "Yes, that is correct my dear, but I'm afraid that Mr Groshny is renting it until the end of the month then he is returning to Russia". "Oh, I am sorry, I thought the gentleman was Gary Williams, he didn't sound Russian". "Mr Groshny is definitely Russian but he did speak perfect English". "I may have misunderstood him, we met in a nightclub and it was very loud". I had what I needed so thanked the Major and hurried back down the path to the car. So, now I knew his real name was Groshny so in my mind, that plane being blown up was meant for me. I sat in the car and cried; how could I fight these people? They had everything off me and now they wanted my life.

The drive back to Cornwall wasn't the best, my head was spinning, when would they try again, I thought? Back in my apartment, Julie and Helen had gone out so I made a coffee and a sandwich and headed to the bedroom to try and research who the hell Groshny was in Russia. It wasn't long until I came across a story and this shocked me. Arvid's real name was Arvid Groshny, brother to the guy I knew as Gary who was actually Ristov Groshny and they were part of a family, of which Michael, who I saw in prison, was actually Michael Groshny.

The article went onto say that they were a feared gang in Russia and arch enemies of the Schultz family. Now it was beginning to fall into place. I'm guessing this family knew I bumped of the head of the Schultz family and decided they would take over, but this time, knowing I was capable of killing, they decided to get in first but they clearly could not take a chance of keeping me alive. My big worry was that they blew the plane up with one of their own on, it was obvious they would stop at nothing. I had to find a way of getting to them first or I was a sitting duck. But how?

THE STUNNER 4

I heard Julie and Helen come back, they were giggling so must have been out for a drink. There is nothing worse than being sober around people that have had a few and especially now that I had this on my mind. I popped down and had one drink with them but decided I would talk to them in the morning, I had to get my thinking cap on if I was going to survive this.

It was 2.00 a.m. .and I hadn't slept a wink when suddenly it came to me. Back in Yorkshire, dad had an Irish friend called Bartley Dunn. I used to think he was so funny and I always called him Bartman after the Simpsons. He would laugh and always enjoyed the craic.

THE STUNNER 4

One night, dad sat me and mum down and told us the story of Bartley Dunn. Bart, as dad called him, had been an explosive expert for the IRA, he and dad became friends through their love of cars. Apparently, Bart was released from the Maze prison in Ireland on the understanding that he had a sponsor. Dad volunteered and they became very big friends. Dad said if ever me or mum needed anything, we were to contact Bart and he would help us. Could he help me now with his contacts I thought? It was maybe a long shot and maybe he wasn't still alive but I had to try. I left Cornwall and headed for Heathcliff, I remembered where Bart lived because of the house name, the previous tenants had called it "LOVE SHACK", mum used to always be taking the mickey about it.

THE STUNNER 4

I arrived in Heathcliff at 8.45 a.m. and noticed I had seven missed calls from Julie so I pulled up outside the neat council house and rang her. "Are you o.k. mate? We have been worried about you". "Yes, I'm fine, I'm quite sure that plane that blew up was meant for me so I can't endanger you and Helen so I am going to go to ground for a while".

"Are you sure you are o.k."? "Yes, tell Helen as well, don't contact me, I will contact you. Love you both" and I hung up.

I opened the little green gate to the path that led up to the house with its wooden plaque with the words Love Shack carved in it and knocked on the door. "Bloody Hell, Saron"!! Bart hadn't changed much other than his hair was grey and he had one of those goatee beards. He hugged me like a long-lost daughter. "Come in lass. Do you want a tea or glass of something stronger"? "Best have a tea Bart with driving".

"Hey lass, this is a lovely surprise". "How's Bridget"? "Oh, you wouldn't know, I lost her two years ago now". "Oh, I am sorry" I could see poor Bart was still hurting, his eyes glazed over.

"So, what are you doing with yourself, you married"? "No". I didn't go into details, besides, I needed to know a bit more of his past. "Is it true you were a member of the IRA Bart"? "I was and still am I suppose, why do you ask"? "Well, dad said if I ever needed anything and he wasn't about I was to see Bart". "That's true lass, I told your dad that and I meant it".

"Dad told me you were an explosives expert". "Not sure about an expert but I was pretty dam good, why, do you want to blow somebody up"? and he laughed, his rosy, red cheeks enjoying the craic, as they call it. "Actually, I do Bart". He almost choked on his tea, "Are you serious"? "Yes, I am Bart, I just need some lessons from you, nobody will know". "Lass, I'm not bothered, they can do what they like with me, I only have six to 12 months left at best, the doctor told me yesterday. I would die a happy man if I can help the daughter of my best friend get out of a bad situation".

THE STUNNER 4

"You are so kind Bart and I am so sorry you are poorly". "Don't worry, since I lost Bridget, I have nothing left so I don't mind going out with a bang. You probably don't know this but your father signed my release papers from the Maze and it was on the understanding that I had a job and all those other things, it was your dad, and to some degree your mum, who helped me. They never judged what I did, in fact, your dad read a lot on Irish history and I think to some degree understood the struggle. So, anything you want, you just have to say, and I mean anything".

"Thank you, Bart". I told him the story about Russia, about my fortune being taken off me and the attempts on my life culminating in the aeroplane being blown up.

"Saron, you have come to the one-stop-shop, I have a lot of contacts in Russia and although it won't be easy to get this scum, I can do it". "Bart, I don't expect you to do it, just teach me and give me the tools to do it".

"We do this together, it will take meticulous planning because we also need to find the document you signed and get your money back". I could not believe what I was hearing. I felt such a heavyweight being lifted off me.

"Right, Saron, first things first, you will need to stay here with me, it will take six to eight months to sort the detail. We will then have to go to Russia. I can get us special papers to enter so don't worry about that. One thing is these people are looking for you. Your only contact is me, smash your phone up now and we will get you a pay as you go. You must follow my rules if you want to be free of this situation". I did what he asked, I knew he was professional. I felt bad about Julie and Helen and the Bistro, I just hoped they understood.

Bart nipped out for a take-away, he was a bit stunned when I said I was a veggie but said Lily Basket down the road did veggie take-outs as well. Before he went, he showed me my room which was plain but clean and tidy.

THE STUNNER 4

I was so pleased I had somebody on my side and especially a trained professional who had Russian contacts.

Over our supper, mine consisted of hommity pie and salad and Barts was fish, chips and mushy peas, we discussed everything. I gave Bart the names of Michael and Arvid Groshny, he wrote them down and said he would do some digging with his contacts.

"Over the coming months, I will train you on what exactly we may have to do, some of it won't be pretty Saron". "Don't worry Bart, if it's against those two, anything we do to them I can stand". He smiled. "You really remind me of your dad, he was a great man Saron". I remember thinking how proud I was of my dad.

"Look Saron, I feel a bit shattered so please don't think I am not enjoying your company but I need to get to bed".
"That's fine Bart, if it's o.k. can I make a drink and watch a bit of T.V"? "Of course, treat the place like your own". He was such a lovely guy.

Chapter 6

Over the next few months, he taught me a lot, he said we would need a pencil bomb, which was basically a bomb-shaped like a thick pencil that was magnetic, but you will hear more of that later.

He also taught me how to use a gun properly. I hoped he would be well enough to help me in Russia.

It was about four months after I arrived on his doorstep that he had news from his contacts about the Groshny brothers. "They are a real bad lot Saron and very dangerous". At first, when Bart was telling me, I thought he was going cold on the idea. I needn't have worried; he was well up for it but said we need to be well planned. October 18th was the planned date. Although nervous, I was also excited, if this all worked out, I was free and if we got the signed papers back, I might get some of my wealth back but that was just a bonus, my freedom was worth more.

Bart said he knew a film make-up artist we should use because my appearance had to be different. He arranged for this guy to come to the house and said he would measure me up for a face mask fitting. Well, that went over my head but Bart seemed to know what he was doing.

The night before I was to have the guy sort the mask, Bart told me more about him and dad. There was so much that dad never spoke about. Dad never mentioned his mum and dad, I did ask mum once but she said dad lost his parents when he was young and his aunty in Yorkshire brought him up. It only clicked when she said her name, Molly Leila. Bart said dad's proper name was Docherty, that grandad Jack Docherty had been killed during the Easter Uprising in Ireland in 1916 so grandma was left to bring up dad and his brother on her own. Apparently, it was so tough that he was sent to Molly Leila to be brought up and from what Bart said he never knew the truth until he was twenty-seven.

"Me and dad were so close Bart but he never told me". "He never told anyone Saron, not even your mum". "Why, was he ashamed or something"? "No, it wasn't that but he always said it was best to let sleeping dogs lie".

THE STUNNER 4

I was now very intrigued by dad's decision to keep his family under wraps but I certainly wasn't ready for the next revelation from Bart.

"I have poured you a strong drink, sit down, I have something else to tell you". "Blimey, I'm sure I can take any more shocks" and I laughed.
"When your dad sort of became my sponsor after I was let out of the Maze, he sorted me somewhere to live and got me a job, the reason being, I am your dad's brother". I nearly dropped the large brandy Bart had given me.

"Oh wow, so you are uncle Bart"? "I guess so Saron. I never told my wife and your dad never told your mum, they thought we were just good friends".

THE STUNNER 4

Maybe I have a bit of dad in me, after all I was thinking, with all this cloak and dagger stuff.

"Tomorrow we will get your disguise sorted then Kevin, another associate, will sit with us and get new passports and visas for our little trip".

"How do we get the bomb out there"? "Don't worry, my colleagues will build it there Saron, we just have to make sure we get in the country ourselves".

"Are you feeling o.k. Bart"? I noticed he was very pale. "Yes, I am having a check-up next Monday before we fly to Russia". "I will go on my own if you are not well enough". "No matter what the doctor says, I am coming with you. I promised your dad I would be here for you". "Dad wouldn't expect that Bart". "He might not but a promise is a promise Saron, and, if nothing else, I pride myself on being a man of my word". The more time I spent with Bart the more he reminded me of dad.

The following day a man and a woman came to model my face, they said they would make my nose wider my cheeks fuller and I would have lines on my forehead and around my eyes that would age me. They took about seven hours and said it would be ready for the weekend so that Saturday we could get the fake passport and visas done.

I lay in bed that night knowing that the following week we would be going back to Moscow and my meeting with Michael and Arvid, or, as Bart had renamed them, Brezhnev and Gorbachev.

I know that as you are reading this you think I must be nuts but this really was a case of kill or be killed and I had no intention of being killed. Saturday soon came around and the passport man and woman came, I had my new full latex head mask on, truthfully, it was incredible, even I didn't know me! They took a few snaps and Bart said for some reason Tuesday was the day to go, I was guessing he had a connection in immigration in Russia so no questions would be asked.

The passports were back to us by Sunday. I was Yvonne Standing, strange name I thought. My visa said I was a dress designer from York, it was amazing, the paperwork, apparently, I worked for a big fashion house and had won all sorts of awards.

I was beginning to feel nervous but so thankful I had Bart, this was going to shape the rest of my life. I so wanted to contact Julie and Helen but I knew I couldn't, I promised myself when this was over, I would treat them. They had been so understanding over all this.

We were flying Tuesday morning from Heathrow so I said we should go down the night before and stay at a hotel, Bart agreed it would be sensible. Our flight was at 11.15 a.m. so we decided to meet for breakfast. I went down expecting Bart to be like all men working his way through the English breakfast buffet but there was no sign of him. I sat and had a croissant and yoghurt while I waited for him.

When he hadn't arrived at 8.40 a.m. I thought I had better go and give him a shout. I arrived at the door and knocked, "Bart, are you up"? I hollered, he said the doors open so I went in, he was in the bathroom fully clothed but was just coughing and almost choking. "Are you o.k."? When he turned around, he had blood on his lips and the sink was awash with blood. "They told me that near the end of my time this would start Saron". "Well, that's it, you are going home, I will do this myself". "I told you lass I was doing this and I am, this isn't going to beat me. I'm made of sterner stuff lass".

What was I putting this man through? It made my hatred of the Russian brothers more intense. Heathrow Security asked a lot of questions but eventually, we were through and on our way but poor Bart, he looked dreadful with no colour at all.

Arriving in Moscow, I had forgotten how cold it really was and I can't say I was pleased to be back, I just wanted my revenge then to get out of the place. What I didn't know was that Bart had other plans. That night we met with Alex Frishtov and another guy who looked so menacing he just mumbled his name so I didn't have a clue.

THE STUNNER 4

This was when the plan was revealed. Apparently, I was to go as Saron to a club called the Ace of Spades where the Groshny brothers went every Thursday, Alex was quite sure they would grab me and take me in their car but Alex, Bart and the nasty guy, would have bumped off the driver then they would follow with the nasty guy driving. I dressed all sexy and headed for their table, they were smoking cigars and quaffing champagne.

When Arvid saw me, he couldn't believe his eyes, he shouted something in Russian and two big guys carried me kicking and screaming throwing me in the back of the waiting car, Michael got one side and Arvid the other then they set off, Alex and Bart followed discreetly until we came to a quiet part of the road.

Then nasty guy pulled up sharply and pointed a gun at each of the brothers. By now Bart and Alex had caught up.

Alex said something in Russian and they got out of the car then Bart said follow them as they bundled them into Alex's car, we must have driven for an hour, the nasty guy never spoke then we went down into a forest and eventually came to what I think we would call a hunter's cottage, the men were secured on chairs. "Go and sit in the car Saron, you don't want to see this". The nasty guy laid out what looked like a roll full of surgeon's tools onto an old table. "Saron, please go now, please" Bart said. "No, I want these to suffer like I did". Arvid started begging for his life, Michael on the other hand just laughed at Alex.

THE STUNNER 4

"So, we have a hard man, do we? Let's see", he picked up the knife and cut Michael's left ear off then stuffed it in his mouth. "Tell me what you want" Arvid pleaded. "Our men won't be far behind you. Our cars have trackers". "Oh, you mean this"? and Bart showed him a black box, "Don't worry, the transmitter bit is back there, an hour away, did you think we were that stupid? We want Saron's money for your life Arvid, fair exchange I believe that was the deal, hard man Michael gave Saron in prison so I will give you the same option. First of all, what do you have and where is it"? "It's back at the house, there is about a million left and deeds to some cottage in a place called Polruan in the U.K".

"Before we go anywhere, Bart here wants you to know something Michael, Bart, let our Hard Man know something before we go for Saron's money".

"Well, you see, it's like this Michael, you lost one ear so I should really balance that up, you are a heap of rotting sewerage" and Bart sliced his other ear off to Michael's screams. "Not so hard now are we, Hardman"? "Let me get a cloth". "No, leave it Saron, if he bleeds to death, he deserves it. Bart, make sure he is secure". "He won't escape from this matey". "Come on then, let's go, grab Arvid, Saron, you can come or stay here". "I'll stay". "Well, here" and he handed me a gun, "If he tries anything, shoot him".

THE STUNNER 4

They left, leaving me with Michael, still bleeding from his wound inflicted on him by Bart. His arrogance hadn't waned though. "So, the beautiful Saron thinks she is going to get her money back and cross me? You have made a massive mistake, your friends will return empty handed but my men will return with them, then we will torture you all before killing you English pigs".

To be honest, he seemed very confident, I was just hoping Bart was going to hold up and the other guys could do the job. Almost nine hours passed when the door burst open, it was Bart, "Come now, give me the gun, he turned and shot Michael in the head. "You o.k. Bart "? "I'll explain, Alex and Ristov are waiting, we have to go now".

THE STUNNER 4

Ristov was a different person, he was laughing and joking, I guess he must have been nervous. "Saron, we made Arvid sign the papers transferring the deeds for your cottage back to you. In the holdall is about the equivalent to one million, eight hundred thousand, I suggest we give Alexander Ristov three hundred thousand each then the Russian guy who lets us on the plane will need one hundred thousand to turn a blind eye and my contact at Heathrow". "That's fine by me Bart, what about you"? "I don't have long so money is no good but knowing my niece is safe and secure, then I have kept my promise to my brother".

I gave the money to Alex and Ristov and thanked them, then me and Bart were ushered through customs onto the plane, they didn't even check our passports but Bart said it would be best to put my disguise on while on the plane just in case Heathrow picks us up on CCTV.

On the plane, Bart told me what had happened that day at the Groshny mansion. He said they killed twelve men then, once they got the money, they tortured Arvid into signing over the cottage in Polruan then Bart said Alex poured fuel over him and burnt him alive, apparently a common thing with the gangs in Russia.

I wasn't sure I wanted that for Arvid, I felt nothing towards horrible Michael but Arvid I would have just shot dead.

We were son through Heathrow and we met the guy who got us through the airport at Watford services. Bart gave him his money and he was soon gone which made us both smile. Back at Bart's house the next day, he wasn't well and within a few days he was so ill he had laid on the settee I sat watching this poor man deteriorate in front of my eyes. The following morning, he could hardly talk but asked me to hold his hand, within twenty minutes he had gone.

I'm not an overly emotional person but I spent the day pretty much in bits, this man had done so much for me and I felt empty, it was like I had lost dad all over again.

The following day, I knew I had to pull myself together. I was a rich girl again so needed to get this money in my bank account and arrange Barts funeral. I paid the council rent for one more month to ensure I got everything squared away.

The funeral was set for the following Tuesday so I set about going through his things to see if he had any friends or even relatives who may want to attend the funeral. After two days of searching, I had turned up nothing. Bart had been a very organised man, just like dad it must be in the genes!!

With nobody to invite there was little point in having the usual sandwiches at a pub, I would be on my own so I decided after the funeral I would hand the keys into the council offices and head for Cornwall to surprise Ju and Helen.

THE STUNNER 4

The day arrived and I had chosen a simple cremation, there was only me there, even the vicar seemed a bit surprised as he stood at the front to say a few words.

"Bartley Dunn was a man of very high principles and integrity, his life had seen many ups and downs and when he lost his wife Bridget, I remember he told me that he was looking forward to the day he would be again by his side. That day has arrived, we will sing Danny Boy, a personal favourite of Bartley's". During the second verse, the curtains closed and that was the end of Barts life. A bit sad I thought but now he was with Bridget.

THE STUNNER 4

I thanked the vicar and put a twenty-pound note in the collection before stepping outside into the crisp winter air.

Walking to my car, two men stepped out from a side path and joined me with one on either side. The first guy spoke.

"Don't be fearful Saron, my name is Lennox and this is my colleague George" and they both handed me their cards, to my utter shock and disbelief they were MI 6 operatives. "We would like to discuss some things with you over a coffee". I was intrigued so agreed, we drove to a little café called Amy's Coffee House.

Over a coffee, they told me they knew all about me and also knew that the Groshny brothers had been murdered, then they said I was implicated. I started to try and wriggle out of this then Rick, one of the guys said, please don't insult us and he turned to the guy who he called Max to show me, they had a big thick file on me going back to Luca.

"You see Saron, you have been on our radar for a very long time but we are offering you a get-out clause". "What do you mean"? "Well, we would like you to join MI 6, if you choose not to, then the other option we have is to let the word out in Russia where you were or we can prosecute you, it's entirely up to you. Being a fair guy, contact us next week with your decision". "O.K.". "Oh, and please don't think you can walk away from this so please contact me". With that, they both left with my life back in turmoil. I sat and finished my coffee then headed to Cornwall and my friends who I missed so much.

The drive to Cornwall had me thinking that it appeared I had little choice and how was I going to tell Julie and Helen that the next season again I would not be involved?

The cafe was all locked up so I put my stuff in my apartment and went back down just as Ju and Helen came in. Julie ran to me. "Saron, Helen look who's here" hugs all around. "Come on Ju, crack the wine and Saron can tell us what happened".

I started and I could see Helen was shocked at what I did, just to get revenge, as she put it. "Tell you what Ju, I hope I never get the wrong side of Saron" and Helen laughed. With the girls now up to speed I dropped the bombshell. "Oh, bloody hell mate, you always said your life was like a game of snakes and ladders, what are you going to do"?

I have little or no choice girls, these are serious people. I have a week to decide but in reality, there is no choice. There is one good thing, you two can have the café back, I'm moving back to Polruan and the cottage and I am going over tomorrow".

The wine flowed and we got more drunk, well, Julie and I did, Helen, the beer monster must have hollow legs the amount she can consume and still be fine the next day!!

THE STUNNER 4

I cleaned my apartment out and headed for Polruan, me and the girls decided we would meet at The King of Prussia in Fowey for a meal on Thursday night. I left the café and headed for Polruan.

I arrived at my cottage and it was desperately in need of some TLC so I decided to get the decorators and carpet people in while I am still here.

I go it all sorted by Tuesday, it was chaos but I didn't mind, I wanted it nice for after I had done my stint with MI6. I had decided I would say I would do two years, I figured they had something planned for me and, as you know, Saron isn't backwards at coming forward!!

THE STUNNER 4

Me and the girls had a meal on Thursday and I had planned to drive to London the next day to MI 6 Headquarters.

Ju and Helen were already sat at a table overlooking the beautiful Estuary. If I am being honest, I could have possibly done without this tonight with the drive up to London the following day. "So, what are we having girls"? "Sorry to be a dry bread but I've got to drive up to London tomorrow so I'll just have a sparkling water please". Then we looked at the menu. For me, it had to be the mushroom Cianly which is mushrooms in white wine and cream with carrots, peas, aubergine and cauliflower over a bed of boiled rice. It was absolutely scrumptious.

THE STUNNER 4

We had a lovely night, we were such good friends and I hated having to leave again but there was no choice.

Chapter 7

The following morning, I set off for the MI 6 building on the banks of the Thames. It was a bit like a large library, busy with people everywhere scurrying about not talking.

I was met at the desk by Sir Gavin Clearmont, he took me into a side room and introduced himself formally. I was about to say my name but he stopped me. "No need my dear, I know who you are. In fact, I probably know more about you than you do yourself" and he smiled.

"I am only doing this for a maximum of two years Mr Clearmont". "All I will say to that is, once you are in, you won't want to leave but I will make a note of your request". "This isn't a request, I want you to sign something". "Well, if you insist my dear. We have booked you into the Hilton which is just down the road whilst you are training". "Training, what do you mean"? "If you are going into the field you will need to be trained with firearms and combat training".

It started to sink in with me that this was for real, that night at the hotel I didn't sleep well thinking about what Clearmont had told me.

The next day, back at MI 6, I was given clearance, Clearmont had drafted an official letter stating that they would have no hold on me after this term of two years so I signed. "O.k. next door are two of your colleagues, Matthew and Paris, they will explain the mission then will start your training".

Matthew was a good-looking guy, I would think late twenties. Paris was also striking in her looks, she had a black dress and her jet-black hair pulled tight in a bun, a bit like those girls in the Robert Palmer video, addicted to love.

"Take a seat" Matthew said as he introduced himself and Paris. "We will be your contacts whilst you are in Spain". "Spain"? "Yes, let me explain, after your training you have to infiltrate Caspian Seeburg, he is probably the biggest drug smuggler in Europe, we have to find his contacts, warehouse etc and that's where you come in, he has an eye for a pretty girl and you are certainly that Saron". I knew my looks and figure would get me into trouble one day I thought.

"So, this is what happens, you sign up under the Official Secrets Act which basically means you can't discuss what you do with anyone from the time you sign, then you will be taken to one of our training camps where you will be taught mortal combat. You will train with an elite firearms instructor then you will meet up with your colleagues, you will all have fake names, passports etc. You must never, and I mean never, disclose your real name or where you are from. This is for your own safety. Sadly, you will learn not to trust anybody, that way you will survive.

So, sign up and let's get you sorted". I signed the papers without reading them, I had this one thing to do then I could get back to normal. "Nice name Saron". "Thank you".

"Here is your new passport". I opened it and they had called me bloody Charlotte, I soon shortened that to Charli!

"Right, let's go next door to meet your colleagues". Ingrid shook my hand, she was only about five feet tall and quite a plain girl. "This is Andy" he was about six foot two and quite handsome "And this is your contact in Spain, Alfredo". Alfredo was in his mid-fifties I guessed, he was quite portly with a droopy moustache, he reminded me of those Mexican cowboys in the John Wayne films that dad used to have me watch every Sunday night when I was about eleven.

"Ok, you three, you will be taken to a secret location for your training. Please remember, you have all signed the Official Secrets Act and are now duty-bound not to converse with anybody in regard to your mission, your identity or who you work for, are we all clear"? We all said yes like some kind of android sheep. The reality was we didn't actually know much about the mission, well, at least I didn't.

We all went in a Range Rover with all the windows blacked out, it was a weird feeling not being able to see where we were going. It must have been almost four hours later when we arrived at our destination.

We were on moorland in what appeared to be a World War two complex with old buildings and tin huts.

The driver instructed us to follow him to the canteen where we were fed and for the first time, I got a feeling for my two colleagues and Alfredo. Ingrid was the quiet, studious type. Andy was a whinger, complaining about everything. Alfredo didn't say anything but just constantly ate.

Next, we were introduced to two army type lads Sergeant Goodson and Sergeant Drake. Drake was bloody gorgeous and I could see straight away he was taking an interest in me.

THE STUNNER 4

"O.k. lovely people, follow me and Sergeant Drake to the gym". The gym was state of the art, nothing like the exterior suggested.

There were four big blue mats and we were each given some kind of Judo suit to put on. I'd done a bit of Judo when I was eight for about two years so I knew how to fall which I was guessing was going to be helpful over the coming weeks.

I assumed they would instruct us and then we would have a go against each other. Well, I got that totally wrong! Goodson pitched in against Andy, poor bloke, and threw him all over the mat. Then Ingrid had a go with Goodson, he was a bit easier on her, but not much.

THE STUNNER 4

Drake had clearly saved me for himself although I didn't mind, he smelt gorgeous close-up. I wanted to ask him what aftershave he was wearing but thought I'd best not. We started and he was going easy on me pulling himself close to me. I wasn't complaining, he was just downright fit as Helen would have said.

He played with me a bit before dropping me on my back then sitting on me. Talk about bloody erotic. Out of earshot, he told me to leave my mobile number on top of my locker and he would call me.

I wasn't really shocked, I knew he had the hots for me from when I first saw him in that room. Later that night, I was in bed wondering if he would call me and, sure enough, he did. "You get time off at the weekend, we aren't supposed to go off the base" but he said Goodson would cover it and we would walk down to the beach then head in to Mellia, he said he knew a great Mexican restaurant and we could have a meal.

By Saturday, all three of us were getting quite handy at this combat discipline and whilst I felt a bit battered and bruised, I wasn't going to miss a day out with the trouser snake Mr Drake. Well, would you!!

He had said to meet him at the last shed at the bottom of the camp and Goodson would let us out. I realised as I stood waiting for him, I didn't know his name, I only knew him as Sergeant Drake or Trouser snake as I called him. I was smiling to myself, I bet it was Francis or hissing Syd. Just then he came around the corner of the building. "What's making you smile Charli"? "Oh, nothing" I said, feeling my face going redder by the minute.

"Thank you, Sergeant Goodson," I said, he smiled that knowing smile as he lets us out. We walked down some wooden makeshift steps then onto a glorious beach although it was quite cold and blustery. We talked as we went along. "You will like this Mexican restaurant". Oh crap, I never told him I was veggie. "What is your Christian name"? "Mark, but everyone calls me Frank, for obvious reasons". I nearly fell over laughing, good job I had taken my stilettos off to walk across the sand or I would have been over. "Well Frank, I'm a veggie". "I know". "How do you know"? "I know more about you than you know about yourself" which seemed a bit eery to be honest.

We climbed back up some steps into Mellia, what a lovely little town, it reminded me of York a bit with its cobbled streets.

"This is it Charli, Mama Sita's, this Mexican has been in their family for four generations, you will love this". I had really got dressed up for this night, my legs, which are a major attribute, certainly caused a stir with my checked mini skirt, stockings and a pale blue, off the shoulder mohair jumper with my Christian Le Boutin black stiletto's.

THE STUNNER 4

We sat at a lovely table, the place was quite busy but the young Mexican girl was very attentive to Frank. I wondered if he took all the girls here but then, what the hell, I fancied the pants off him.

The veggie menu was excellent and I chose rice and carrot parcels to start then vegetable risotto with a pea and cauliflower puree. Frank, being a roughty tufty soldier went for the Tomahawk steak. I was a bit surprised with it being a Mexican but apparently, the steak was the house speciality. Frank started to tell me his life story, how he had now been in the army for twenty years, twelve of them in Special Forces. He said he had been divorced twice, the first marriage lasted eleven months, the second two and half years and that he had a daughter of eighteen but he never saw her, he said her mum had poisoned her against him. I guess all men say that I thought.

Our starters came and he started to ask me questions. "So, Charli". "That bloody name"! I really was pleased with that but I wondered if this was a test. "Where are you from"? I looked into his beautiful blue eyes and just said, sorry I can't reveal any details to you. He never questioned my reply which kind of made me think it was a bit of a set-up.

The rest of the night was really good, at around 10.30 p.m. they cleared the table and they had a lookalike Michael Bublé singing so he asked me to dance. When I say this guy was gorgeous, he really was and he smelt so good. At midnight, we started walking back and he insisted on giving me a piggyback across the sand with me holding my stilettoes.

Sergeant Goodson let us back in and we walked up to my room. I so wanted to ask him to come in but luckily, he asked if I was inviting him in for a nightcap.

We had just got through the door when we were virtually ripping the clothes off each other, his eyes almost went out on sticks when he saw my pale blue lacey lingerie set with stockings, I kept my heels on, I knew men liked that. We fore played for a good half hour, his toned body pressing against mine. He did things you could only dream of and never seemed to tire before eventually, I had fulfilment then he did. Gentleman to the end I said which made him smile.

Afterwards, he said he'd best go otherwise he would lose his job and I might end up locked up. We kissed passionately as he left and he gave me a playful tap on my bum cheeks. That night I lay on the bed exhausted but contended.

We had a further two weeks of combat training and, though I say it myself, I felt good, the only problem was Sergeant Goodson took us and I never saw Frank, I thought about asking Goodson but if he had dumped me or used me I wasn't going to give him the pleasure.

At the end of the two weeks, we did open arm knife training for ten days then we were told we were moving for artillery training, this time they told us it would be in Catterick. I hadn't got to know Ingrid or Andy, they seemed to have something going on so I kept my distance. On the ride up to Catterick, it kind of annoyed me that Trouser Snake had disappeared into thin air after one night of passion. I know what you are thinking, Saron is losing her touch. I'll be back I promise.

The accommodation in Catterick was loads better, in fact, it was quite nice. That night we met our three instructors. Barry Harris introduced himself as small arms and grenades expert. Bloody hell I thought, grenades? I didn't expect that. Then there was Jackie Curzon, she said she would be teaching us bomb disposal. Bloody hell, it gets worse I thought. They saved the best for last, wait for it, Ronnie

170

THE STUNNER 4

Whiteboard stood up and looked quite a surly man. "My job will be to teach you to handle torture".

I think Ingrid, Andy and I thought we didn't sign up for this. "O.K. you lot, enjoy your meal, the real work starts tomorrow. Breakfast at eight o clock in the morning here where I will meet you for your first lesson".

That night I was beginning to realise that we weren't playing at this, the training they were giving us clearly meant bad things may happen.

We were halfway through our breakfast when Barry Harris came in, he never spoke, just walked off, picked up a bowl of cereal and Greek yoghurt and sat on his own. By now we had all finished and we're sitting like space cowboys waiting for some instruction from Harris. Eventually, he finished. "Follow me" he barked. We followed him all the way up the camp and into a padded, very large room. Laid out on a table were all types of guns, even machine guns and the dreaded hand grenades. "What do we call you"? Ingrid said. "Barry is fine. O.K., do any of you know anything about guns"? "I used to shoot clay pigeons at the weekend" Andy told him.

"Well, you can forget all that rubbish, clay pigeons don't fire back. The first lesson is to be aware of your surroundings, stay calm, even under pressure, that way, your hands will stay calm. Keep focused, remember, it's kill or be killed, that is the simplest choice.

THE STUNNER 4

Right, Mr Claypigeon man, step up here. Pick a gun you fancy. No, tell you what, feel them all then choose the one that feels right for you". There must have been at least twenty. After looking and feeling them all, he chose his gun. "Not a bad choice Andy, a Beretta 85 Cheetah. A bit flash I might say so I hope you didn't pick the gun that could one day save your life just on looks. O.k., sit down with your gun, it isn't loaded so we are o.k. Ingrid, you choose". I could see Ingrid was nervous as she approached the overwhelming amount of guns. She tried them all then chose a Random 85 then I chose a 9 mm Baretta. I felt a bit like the chosen one when Harris was telling the other two I had chosen the best gun on offer.

THE STUNNER 4

"Right, down there are your targets, we don't leave here today until you all have one bull's eye". He then showed us how to hold the guns and fire.

Daft as it might seem, the first hour, none of us was hitting the target but then we began to hit it, Andy was first with a bull's eye which I was pleased for him as Harris had given him stick. Ingrid was next then after four and a half hours finally did it.

"O.k. well done all of you, now I will show you how to clean your chosen weapon, ensure you clean your gun after every use. This could save your life remember".

By 6.00 p.m. that night I felt shattered, my arms ached from holding the pistol so

174

THE STUNNER 4

I was pleased when he said let's call it a night, same time in the canteen tomorrow.

I think we all needed an early night. I decided a nice soak would be advisable ready for the next day and what that had in store for us

The following morning was the same ritual, we were having breakfast, Harris came in ten minutes after us, ate his breakfast then took us for training. We spent a full week trying to hit bulls' eyes then he explained to us the dangers of the hand grenade-like we needed to know, it's a flipping bomb and the only thing stopping it from going off in your hand is a flipping pin!

THE STUNNER 4

In total, we had a month with Harris. I was beginning to wonder if we would ever learn enough.

We were handed over to Jackie Curzon, she was actually quite nice, different to Harris. We apparently were to work a week with her, she said she would train us on real bombs, she explained that if she didn't, we wouldn't be nervous and she had to gauge everything, especially our hands which mustn't shake. We were doing things like you did at fairs as a child, a wire where you take a looped wire around a circuit without it alarming.

It seemed quite easy after the Harris course, that was until the last day, we were to disarm a bomb each. Ingrid did hers quite quickly, that left me and Andy.

THE STUNNER 4

I was sweating so much, we had ten
minutes left when Andy did his, that just
left me. It's crazy, all that training and
my mind had gone blank, was it the blue
wire or the green? I closed my eyes and
went for green. There was a loud bang, I
thought I had died, all I could see was
white dust everywhere then I heard
everyone laughing. "You're not dead
Charli, it's a flour bomb". Talk about
relieved. I wasn't bothered about being
the class clown just happy I was alive.
"Don't worry, we always get one who
sets the flour bomb off.

We were told that the next week would
be very tough and asked if anybody
wanted to leave, but of course, that didn't
run to me I had a deal with them.

THE STUNNER 4

Apprehension kicked in when Ronnie Whiteboard met us in the canteen for breakfast, he seemed a nice guy, I got that totally wrong. First thing he did was split us up, I never saw Ingrid or Andy again, not that we had become friends or anything but I did feel alone now. Whiteboard explained the stages of torture and how to rise above the pain and the constant questioning. He taught me about OBE, sorry that's an Out of Body Experience for you lot.

It was an incredible thing he taught me but he was a snappy guy, if he thought my mind was wandering. He went through the types of torture.

"Listen now Charli because you need to understand, the human mind has long been capable of dreaming up new and terrible ways to punish alleged transgressors, villains, witches, and anyone else who was unlucky enough to be in the wrong place at the wrong time. We're all familiar with the old standbys: hanging, burning, stoning. Yawn. What if someone *really* wrongs you? Like steals your sheep or somehow must have caused a crop failure or something because they gave you a shifty look that one time? Throughout the ages, some extremely brutal methods of torture and execution have come and gone. And there are a few that have not yet gone too like physical torture, deprivation usual sleep, water torture and of course the fear of what your tormentor is going to do to you".

Whilst it was interesting it was also very scary, after three weeks with Ronnie Whiteboard I did wonder what the hell I had agreed to.

The next day I met with Sir Gavin Clearmont and my first operation was explained to me. I was to fly to Marbella and find a way of infiltrating the Caspian Seeburg operation, "And that's where your contacts Matthew and Paris will be available to you, here is a mobile which is also a tracker, Paris' number is under mother and Matthew is under father, just in case. Seeburg visits the Polla Polla bar twice a week and that would be your best chance he has an eye for a pretty girl".

"So, what exactly do you want me to do"? "Once you have familiarized yourself with his operations, we need the following, the drug contacts for the U.K. and who he deals with, and I don't mean at street level, we want the main guy. Any paperwork for hard evidence you can get, I realise that might be difficult, but that would help tremendously in court. Alfredo is your day-to-day contact, he will make himself known to you when you land in Marbella, he will be masquerading as a taxi driver. The only time these two come into play is if things go wrong" and he pointed to Matthew and Paris, "They are highly trained officers and will get you out of there. Charli, this is a massive undertaking and, I won't lie to you, we have been trying to get him for ten years and he is always one step ahead of us, we have lost two well-experienced officers, one last year and one the year before so this is not an easy task.

THE STUNNER 4

O.k., so a taxi will pick you up for the 10.00 a.m. flight from Manchester to Marbella. Good luck Charli". Oh, I just wished I could be called Saron, I really didn't suit the name Charli but I understood why it had to be changed.

I packed my case but struggled to sleep that night. I know fate takes a big part in everybody's life but I did wonder, if I hadn't taken that job in London with Luca and his family, I wouldn't have been doing this now.

THE STUNNER 4

Chapter 8

The following day I flew to Marbella and, true to their word, Alfredo was waiting with my name on a piece of card held aloft. I had to smile, he had a bright yellow Hawaiian shirt on with his trousers held under his quite large belly as if they were hanging on for their life. "Charli , Charli" he shouted and waved.

Let the adventure begin, I just hope I come out of this alive and, to be honest I wasn't sure I would. Alfredo took me to my apartment which was quite nice, he said he had arranged for a cleaner to come in twice a week, Tuesday and Friday, so not to leave anything incriminating out, lock everything in the safe.

THE STUNNER 4

He had left me a bottle of wine so I put on my red bikini, poured myself a glass of wine and departed to the balcony which was a great suntrap. I had three spare days before I was to visit the Pollo Pollo and try and get noticed so a nice tan would help.

After a couple of days, my tan was nicely topped up and have to say, I was quite enjoying the rest after all the trials and tribulations of the training camps. I felt as fit as a butcher's dog. I decided that this was feeling a bit like a holiday so I would nip out for a bar snack. They had purposely rented the apartment close to the Pollo Pollo but there were bars all down this stretch of road so I put on some tight red skinny chinos with an off the shoulder white blouse and, of course, the obligatory Jackie Onassis black sunglasses, and headed out but making sure everything was in the safe neatly locked away.

I looked at a few bars but Marukas steak house looked nice and they did bar snacks. I wished I could send Ju and Helen some pics, the Spanish waiters and bar staff were just gorgeous.

"Good evening pretty lady, I'm Stephano, would you like my special cocktail"? "What is it called and what's in it"? "I call it Sexy Lady so it suits you". Flippin charmer I thought. "It has two measures of vodka, one measure of white rum, one measure of blue Curacao and one measure of brandy, that is to make you a bit randy, sexy lady". He had practised this I thought. "Then we add pineapple and mango". "Go on then Stephano, why not".

It really tasted good and looked good complete with its umbrella and sparkler. I ordered tomato, pesto and goats' cheesecakes and a few cracked potatoes.

The food was fabulous and the view of the little Spaniard wasn't bad. The drink was immense and by the end of the night, three cocktails later, I decided to bale. "Goodnight pretty lady, come and sees Stephano soon" I put my hand up and left.

I had really enjoyed tonight and slept well. The following day I lay out in the glorious weather and tried another bar at night but it wasn't as good as the night before.

The time had come to start work, I wore a tight-fitting Alexander McQueen dress, black sheer stockings and black

THE STUNNER 4

Christian Le Boutin shoes, if this didn't get me noticed nothing would. I arrived at 7.30 p.m. Alfredo said Seeburg arrived at 8.00 p.m. every Tuesday and Thursday. I had my back to the door but overheard the waiter say welcome Mr Seeburg. My heart was racing, I pretended to go to the toilet which meant I had to pass his table. Damn, he had his head turned and was talking, when I came back out, I was shocked, the man I was supposed to be getting close to, Seeburg, was somebody I knew from the time I was living on the island, this guy was a business associate of Lucas and I knew him as Dan Scoobley, or as everybody called him, Scooby.

I tried to briskly walk past but he saw me. "Saron"? and he stood, "Are you on your own"? "Ugh, yes". "Then you must join us, this is Adrianna my daughter, we call her Ady". "Pleased to meet you", she looked very Mediterranean with jet black hair and olive skin, she appeared very quiet but I then realised she was deaf and Scooby was doing sign language.

"What are you up to these days? I heard you sold everything and have become a recluse somewhere at the tip of England". This guy was playing with me, he knew where I lived, I went cold. "Yes, something like that" I said, trying to keep as much of the conversation on him, not me.

"Very sad the situation with Luca, Saron, but the Russians don't forgive and forget". "So, have you retired over here"? "I suppose you could say that, kind of

semi-retired, my wife died four years ago
so me and Ady spend about eight months
here each year, the weather is nice and
the food is good.

You must come up to the villa and have a
meal with us". "Oh yes, that would be
nice". We spent the night doing
pleasantries but all the time I got the
impression that Scooby knew more about
me than he was sharing.

I lay in bed that night thinking this was a
bit unnerving, me knowing him and then
Ady and the sign language. The next day
I would need to tell Alfredo about
Scooby.

The pool was calling after breakfast so I
rang Alfredo, he said he would come over

to discuss, he didn't want to do it over the phone.

Alfredo arrived, not much better dressed than he previously was, we sat at the dining room table and I told him about Scooby. What he said next shocked me, he said MI6 knew his real name wasn't Seeburg, they also knew him as Scooby, until he opened up operations and ran from Spain, they left him alone but now his empire was growing and they needed to bring him down. "Didn't anybody think to tell me about Scooby"? "I have to be honest, it is an internal concern and I will report it but in reality, you have a better chance now of getting us what we need if he has already asked you to his villa". "Well, have you anything else you wish to tell me"?

THE STUNNER 4

Alfredo lowered his head. "Be careful, Adrianna or Ady as you know her is not deaf, they use sign language to communicate, that way nobody knows anything, oh, and she isn't his daughter she is his bodyguard and assassin".

"Oh, great, thanks for that Alfredo". "When are you going to his villa"? "He said next Tuesday, Ady will pick me up". "It's no good you wearing a wire, any conversation of any importance will be done with sign language, Scooby is no fool".

Alfredo left and I now had a week to try and get an angle on sign language, so instead of reading a slushy book I set about learning sign language.

THE STUNNER 4

I was quite surprised, I began picking it up quickly, I just needed to practise which I did in front of the mirror. After four days I was really pleased with my progress and was beginning to get confident that if the word drugs or transport were used, I could get it. By the time the night came around for me to go to the villa I really was feeling quite confident although not very tanned as all my time had been taken up learning sign language.

Ady picked me up, she certainly was strange pretending to be deaf and to think she is a stone-cold killer. Well lady you have met your match I thought. The villa was fabulous but then it would be, this guy was seriously rich when I last knew him. He met me like we were on date night and, to be honest, I would rather ride around Leek on a horse like Lady Godiva than jump into bed with this arse.

He was really playing the gentleman, puling the chair out for me and he had chefs cooking for us. Ady did some sign language and I got it, she said "The movement papers are on your table in your bedroom". "Sorry Saron, Ady isn't stopping for dinner, she is meeting somebody tonight aren't you Ady"? he said when what he actually said was "Tell Tommo he'd better get the bigger shipment over in a fortnight". Got you I thought.

Ady left and Scooby was reminiscing about Luca and how they used to have so many investments, he still carried on with the pretence about Ady. But to be fair, he said he would arrange a taxi back so while he was doing that I said I needed the toilet. My mission is to get a picture of the note that Ady spoke about so I can give it to Alfredo. Scooby told me the toilets were on the second floor then joked they were next to his bedroom so as not to make a smell. Cheeky git.

Now that I knew his bedroom was next door to the toilet, I slipped away while he was sorting the taxi out, I knew I would not have long. The paperwork was sat nicely on his dressing room table. I took a couple of pictures on my phone then nipped to the bathroom to flush the toilet. I kept up the pretence and washed my hands and headed back to the dining table.

THE STUNNER 4

"Your taxi will be here in two minutes. We must do this again Saron, this is my mobile number, give me a call". "Thank you, Scooby, I have enjoyed the evening" and with that, I climbed in the taxi and headed back to my apartment believing I was the next James Bond. The following morning, I rang Alfredo, he said he would be over at lunch.

After a bit of sunbathing, I made a quick Greek salad for us. The doorbell rang and I let Alfredo in.

"You look excited Saron"? "I am, take a look at this". I showed him the arranged time drop off in the port of Marbella and even the boat name, the Lady Casa. "That's brilliant work, well done Saron. I will arrange a S.W.A.T team to take them down then we can arrest the guy you know as Scooby. It's a week from today so plenty of time to get arranged. Thank you for lunch, I will be in touch". Alfredo left and I did my favourite thing, hit the sunbed with a glass of wine and a book. This seemed a lot easier than I had been expecting.

On the day that Alfredo said they had planned to arrest everyone from the note information I gave them, I got a visit. On opening the door two burly guys with greasy long black hair wearing long leather coats pushed me over. One of them pulled a gun, "Get up, sit on the settee" he said. The other one then put gaffer tape across my mouth then bound my feet and hands. He was pointing the gun at me and shouting safe, where is your safe? He grabbed me and made me show him. "Combination, hurry up". "4144" I said then he put the gaffer tape back across my mouth again.

Now I knew I had a problem, my loaded gun and passport were in there. The guy seemed to know what he wanted, he gestured to his mate and they left with my gun and passport.

So, I am on the settee having been robbed and left trussed up like a Christmas turkey waiting to be cooked. Oh, and they took my phone so I am snookered. I have no way of getting hold of Paris, Matthew or Alfredo so now I was in a pickle, as mum used to say.

I had to get my thinking cap on, I couldn't go to the police or the Embassy because my passport wasn't legal, I was just hoping Alfredo would get in touch because he should have been arresting Scooby tomorrow so I decided to sit tight and see what tomorrow would bring.

The following day I really couldn't settle, the apartment had Sky so I put Sky News on just at the right moment, or wrong moment, depending on your viewpoint.

The reporter was standing at the port Of Marbella. "Today, we have seen probably one of the biggest raids by Spanish Police and Special Agents who confiscated a private yacht, only to find that what initially they thought was drug smuggling was actually nothing of the kind" My heart sank, I had been set up, I should have known it was all too convenient

THE STUNNER 4

Scooby knew. I also knew I had to get out of Marbella and in very quick time.

I felt dreadful, I was totally on my own with no money, no cards, no phone and no weapon to defend myself with. But this was to be nothing compared to what was coming down the road.

I threw all my clothes in a suitcase and headed out of the apartment down the stairs and out into the street following the stunning white buildings as far away as I could. For some reason something told me to take a side street halfway down some stone steps, there was only a Pawn Shop, well it had three golden balls and it said: "CASA DE EMPENOS" which at a guess said Pawn something. I went inside and showed the man my Cartier Tank watch, I knew it was worth about six grand, he offered me fifteen hundred euros. I must have smelt of desperation as I took his money. Now I had to get to the airport, get a ticket and get home. Just as I left the pawnshop and climbed the steps to the main street, Scooby and Ady were sitting waiting for me in a big car then two big guys arrived behind me from nowhere. "Get in Saron, we need to talk".

It wasn't said in a way that I had a choice to decline the offer. Scooby didn't say anything else, as we walked into his villa, there on the dining room table was my gun, passport, phone and money. "Sit at the table Saron, we need to talk. You do realise what you did? If it was right, I would have been facing life in prison.

THE STUNNER 4

So, did you think I don't know about you working with the British Government, Charli"? and he laughed? I really knew I was in trouble now, I understood the training but surprises were still to come. Scooby shouted come in my friend I believe you know Saron and in walked bloody Frank! "Our Frank here is a double agent who knows which side of his bread is buttered don't you Frank"? Frank just smiled.

"So, you see Saron, you picked the wrong side and certainly, by trying to set me up, that was not a good career move. I have contacts in the British Secret Service, why do you think I have lasted so long?

I know all about Russia, in fact, there is very little I don't know about you so your torture training is quite useless as there is no need. What I can't have is a rat as an associate so with that in mind you will have to go on your journey to be with Luca", basically, that meant I was about to be killed. "Frank, take the boat, go out to sea, kill her, weight her down and throw her overboard".

I have always been a survivor but was unsure if I could get out of this situation. Frank roughly handled me and took me down to the port. "Frank, you don't have to do this, just let me go, I won't say anything". He just stared at me like he was on a trip.

Once on the boat, it dawned on me that this was the end. He threw me in the hull so he could set off. I think my luck was in, there was a small knife in the kitchen sink, he hadn't tied me up thinking there was nowhere for me to go. I knew he was a big powerful man and if I was to get out of this situation, I had to kill him. I decided I would lie on the bed and as he reached over to get me, I would slit his jugular. For some reason, I didn't feel nervous, apprehensive yes but not nervous, I suppose it was shit or bust as Helen would say.

I heard the engines cut out about thirty minutes into the journey then I heard him coming down. This was it. I took a deep breath and he called me to get off the bed when I didn't move, he came to grab me, this was my one chance. I stuck the knife into his neck, I must have been spot on because blood came pumping out, he screamed, falling backwards trying to pull the knife out of the wound. It was quick, at the most, a minute and a half and he was dead.

Now I had to struggle with him back onto the deck, I managed it but don't ask me how. Once up top I tied anything of weight to him then scrabbled him overboard. Next was to clean the boat of the blood and decide my next move. I headed for Malaga and you may ask how did I sail the boat? Well, to be honest, I don't know, I just did. Needs must as they say.

I managed to get a guy to jump on board at Malaga and park it, I'm sure that isn't the correct terminology but I'm sure you understand.

THE STUNNER 4

The guy said his name was Fabio, he was about the same height as me which would normally put me off, I liked tall guys, he was nice and kind and not bad looking, he asked me if I would like to have a drink with him and some Tapas. I suppose you could say an end to a perfect day, a jug of Sangria, murdered a guy and eating Tapas, bet there is a song in there if any songwriters are reading this.

Fabio was very nice, he said he had owned an engineering company but when his wife died, he sold everything, bought a boat and now sails the Mediterranean. I listened intently thinking, six months away sailing with Fabio that the heat might have died down and maybe I could go back to my life in Cornwall.

THE STUNNER 4

I know what you are thinking, I'm a nut case and maybe you are correct but this was a chance I had to take so I made up a story. I said my husband was a jealous man and because of how I looked I got plenty of male attention and he didn't like it, I said we'd had a massive row and I took the boat, hence the reason I couldn't park it.

Fabio laughed and he had such a crazy laugh it made me laugh. "Saron, you are a crazy lady, come with me, we are going sailing". I put the act on that I couldn't possibly but knowing I definitely would.

We finished our meal and he was a real gent, I got on my boat and he got on his, he then said, "If you want to come with me, I am leaving at 10.30 a.m. in the

THE STUNNER 4

morning, if not, have a wonderful life".
This made my mind up I was going to be
there, come hell or high water.

Chapter 9

The following morning, armed with the clothes I stood up in, I joined Fabio on his boat. Funnily enough, he never asked about my clothes and things until later that day and I explained I had basically run away so these were my only clothes.

"Right then Saron, we will head for Valencia, they have great shops there". "Look, don't think I am being unkind but I only have what you see me in now and I have no money to buy clothes". "Saron, I will buy you clothes, that isn't a problem". "I will pay you back every penny Fabio".

"I can't have a beautiful lady not looking her best now, can I? Do me a favour, go to the fridge and take the top off a lager for us both please". Think I am going to quite like this I thought.

He was great fun and told me he and his wife had wanted children but it never happened. He said he threw himself into building a successful business but hadn't noticed how depressed Isabella, that was his wife's name, had become.

He then told me she committed suicide, he found her after he was late back from a meeting, she had hung herself in the garage. I felt so sorry for him, he said even now he dreads opening a garage door.

It was a couple of days later when we landed in Valencia. Fabio was a really nice man, he never bothered me, he had his bedroom and I had mine.

THE STUNNER 4

"Come on then Saron, let's get you kitted out". The first shop he took me to was Bella Laguza, I knew this was really expensive and really nice but I couldn't expect him to pay these prices.

I explained but he insisted. "Look Saron, I have no children, no wife, it's just me, I sold my company for a lot of money, and I mean a lot of money so I can have what I like, I love your company and I don't say this lightly, you have given me something to look forward to, we will have a great time".

I thought, what the hell, he was a nice guy and if it makes him happy and it gets me out of the way then, why not?

Armed with a load of new clothes, shoes and handbags, we headed back to the boat to change, he wanted to take me to the Casa Faena Restaurant, an Argentinian steak house. "Sorry Fabio. I am vegetarian". "It's not a problem, my wife was also and they have an excellent vegetarian menu".

We walked down the cobbled streets to a beautiful little restaurant all nicely lit up. Fabio was right, it had an excellent veggie menu.

I went for a poached egg on a bed of rocket with parmesan shavings then, for my main, I ordered a cauliflower and cashew nut paella with a beetroot jus, The whole meal was to die for and I was really enjoying Fabio's company, he was such a gentleman in his ways. We had a couple of bottles of red then left. Walking back to the boat, I don't know what came over me but I thanked him then kissed him passionately. The poor man wept. "Oh, I'm sorry Fabio". "It's not you Saron, it's me, I never thought I would be kissed again". "You are silly" and I kissed him again, this time he embraced me. Now we walked back arm in arm and it felt right, back at the boat he was still incredibly kind, I knew I would have to take the lead.

"Come into my bedroom", he wasn't hesitant, just, I guess, overawed. That night we made love, it was mad and passionate but sensual and loving, he made me feel like a real woman.

Afterwards, he said "I think I am falling for you Saron". I didn't know what to say but was quite sure I felt the same. He was everything a girl could want, he was kind, considerate, rich and not bad looking I'm sure my mum would have approved, had she still been alive.

I was feeling so safe and so secure, we had so much fun, stopping at little coves and going up the coast, he said our next big stop was to the Canary Isles. I had heard about them but never been. We decided to stop for three weeks and Fabio was having the boat serviced. We stayed at a place called La Caleta on the southwest coast of Tenerife, it was close to Costa Adeje but not as built up, it had beautiful small restaurants and lovely walks.

THE STUNNER 4

Don't laugh at me but I think I was falling in love and it was a different love to when I was with Luca, that relationship was totally on his terms but this is different, it just feels good.

I had somewhat forgotten about my old life, I knew I couldn't contact Ju and Helen as I was sure MI6 would be staking the place out and possibly Scooby, I had certainly upset a few people.

The three weeks seemed to fly by, I was that happy. With the boat fully serviced, Fabio decided our next journey in my incredible life. "Right, Saron, let's head for Sardinia". "Oooh, that sounds exciting" I said, putting my arms around his waist. For a few days now I had toyed with the idea of telling Fabio everything but I was scared I would lose him, the question is, can you build a relationship on mistrust? Mum always said truth and trust are the two things to always have by your side at all times.

I know what you are thinking, I had hardly followed mums' thoughts, had I? It was quite a calm crossing to Sardinia. Fabio said he knew an Italian family on the island and wanted to introduce me to them. I was a bit apprehensive because clearly, he had been here before with his wife. He said Bollo and Maria were lovely people and would welcome me.

We parked the boat in Sardinia, I am again still not sure of the terminology and were met by Bollo and I assumed Maria. He seemed really pleased to see us, Maria

THE STUNNER 4

made a fuss of Fabio but it was clear from the start she must have been big friends with Fabio's wife and she wasn't going to make it easy for me.

Never mind I thought, I have fallen for this guy and there was no way my happiness was going to be affected by anybody.

Fabio had arranged an apartment for us just down the road from Bollo and Maria's house. I decided I needed to tell him everything otherwise, when asked things over dinner, I would have to lie and I didn't want to do that.

"Bollo, pour us a glass of red, I want to sit and talk to you". "If it's about Maria, don't worry, she will come around". "No,

THE STUNNER 4

it's me Fabio, I want to tell you about me". He looked concerned.

"My name is Saron Leila, I was born in a little village called Heathcliff in Yorkshire". "Why now are you telling me"? "Because you lump, I love you and I want us to be totally honest with each other going forward. When I was a young woman, I applied for a job as a nanny to two children for a family in London. To cut the story short, I ended up with the father of the children, his name was Luca, he was a billionaire and when he died, I was the sole beneficiary but then, organised crime took it off me". All the time I was thinking, do I tell him about the people I have killed? I decided to save that for another day. "Amway, to cut a long story short, I own a house in

THE STUNNER 4

Cornwall and a share in a bistro type place but I have given my share up to my two best friends but, because of circumstances, I haven't signed off on it but I will and I have about one million pounds in my bank account".

I could sense poor Fabio was dying to ask me questions. "About a year back, I was recruited by MI6, the British Secret Service, I was put through training then I had to infiltrate a gang of people but it turned out I knew one and he knew me. They arranged to kill me but I escaped on that boat that you parked for me. So basically, you helped me escape and by the time we return, if we do, I am guessing it will all be over".

THE STUNNER 4

"I am astounded". "I am sorry". "No, don't be, I am not astounded at your life story, I am astounded that you said you love me, somebody as beautiful and caring as you are, I feel very special Saron".

Wow, had I found a gem I thought. I so wanted to take him to meet Ju and Helen, they would love him. He reminded me a bit of dad, I guess that what the first attraction was, before Fabio, I seemed to attract the worst kind. It was a lovely evening as we walked up the road to Bolo's house, I snuggled into Fabio and felt on top of the world.

Initially, Maria was quite frosty but after the lovely meal, Fabio went into the kitchen and when she came back, she was

so different, she actually apologised
saying she was a great friend of Fabio's
wife and she had been shocked to see him
with me but watching the pair of us
together we were both clearly in love and
she raised her glass, "Fabio and Saron". I
could have cried, I could see it meant a
lot to my Fabio.

During the next couple of weeks, we
went fishing, I know, me, fishing, would
you believe it!! Swimming, snorkelling
we had such a fabulous time I never
wanted it to end

Fabio said it was time to move on and
said we would head for Italy.

THE STUNNER 4

I know this might seem silly but I couldn't help worrying, what if Luca's family see me? For the first time I wished I was ugly and not so noticeable.

Fabio said we would dock at the Yacht Club, Marina di Stabia, he said we could moor there for ten days then hire a car and see Italy. It sounded so lovely, I can't explain the feeling of happiness I had.

The marina was beautiful, we had a fabulous meal then stayed the night at the hotel just off the slipway and Fabio ordered a car. I cuddled up to him that night feeling so secure and happy.

The following day, Fabio had hired one of those jeeps where the doors and lid come off and we headed for Naples. I always remember watching that Italian chef, Gino something, and he was from Naples and he said "They say you should see Naples and die" I had no intention of doing the latter but you get my drift.

Naples took my breath away, it was just incredibly lovely, the weather, food and scenery were fantastic, it just had everything and I felt like I had everything. We spent the most fabulous two days in Naples and I can honestly say it is the best place I have ever been to. Now onto Rome, what a place, this was steeped in history.

I felt like bloody Judith Chalmers on Wish you were here. Fabio said this was his first time in Rome so that was good, we were making our own memories, little

THE STUNNER 4

did I know what was waiting for us around the corner.

THE STUNNER 4

Chapter 10

It was 2 .00 a.m. and I had turned over for the umpteenth time, I was always like that if I sensed something was wrong. I slid over to cuddle up to Fabio but he wasn't there so I switched the bedside light on, Scooby was sat in a chair and two of his henchmen had trussed poor Fabio up and were holding a gun on him, my world came crumbling down.

"Hello Saron, I see you have another sucker falling for you". "Please Scooby, let him go, he hasn't done anything". "Did you tell him about poor Frank? Did you really think that you could pull the wool over Scooby and I would just let it go"? He nodded to the man with the gun and he pulled the trigger, shooting Fabio.

THE STUNNER 4

I screamed and ran to his side only for one of these brutes to pick me up and throw me on the bed. The next guy put something across my mouth and I passed out.

They kept me drugged so I had no clue where I was but I was in a basement. Eventually, Scooby came down and introduced me to somebody he called Doctor Fix. This man was quite weasley with a white coat and surgical gloves. "Mr Fix here loves to torture don't you Fixy boy"? the man nodded. "So, to set you off, we will lie you down on this table" and they secured my head in what resembled a vice.

Fix then unrolled tools in a white cloth. they shone. He laid them out so I could see them. "Right Saron, we will leave you alone for 24 hours and then we will talk before Doctor Fix really gets to work".

Suddenly, fix kneeled across me turning on a tap that was dripping very slowly on my forehead. Then they left, laughing and turned the light off. After what must have been five hours, the water felt like it was drilling a hole in my head, I felt so tired and emotional and scared, I tried to remember the training, especially the out-of-body experience.

The following morning a guy came in and turned the tap off, I think he was amazed I wasn't stir crazy. "Do you want a drink"? "Please" I said, hoping he would get me out of the vice. He went off and came back. I noticed he had a handgun. He released me and, although I was groggy, I saw my chance. He poured the tea and I grabbed his gun and whacked him over the head. I knew where I was going, that was to get Scooby, no more running, he killed my Fabio and he has to pay. I could hear his voice once I got out of the basement. As I approached, the other henchman came from nowhere, he grabbed me but I managed to throw him over my shoulder and he landed on the floor dazed. I put two bullets in his head for Fabio, now for Scooby, the TV was on but the window was open, he had gone! I ran and ran, eventually I could see a police car in a layby, I had to take my chance. I told him to take me to the British Embassy, it took a few hand signals and watching my lips but he eventually got it. I was so pleased to get into the Embassy and told them to get hold of Sir Gavin Clearmont, the head of MI6. That certainly got a reaction. They put me in an oak panelled room and I waited for almost an hour before a guy who announced himself as Tarquin Hughes came in. "I believe you told our people you are MI6"? "Yes, that's correct". "Well, I am very sorry, you gave your name as Saron Leila but MI6 have no record of you". "What? Did you speak with Clearmont"?

"I'm afraid we had no joy there but his number two gave me the information". "Get me Clearmont". "My dear, it is useless to get aggressive with me, we have no power over MI6".

THE STUNNER 4

"Look you heap of rotting sewerage, I have a killer after me and this is all because of MI6 and I want this sorting". "Let me try again Saron, just calm down and drink your coffee".

This time the clock said 2.10 p.m. when Hughes left the room and eventually returned at 5.50 p.m. "A message has been sent to Sir Gavin Clearmont and we will have to wait for a reply". If only I had the number of Andrew or Paris, what a complete mess this is.

At just gone 8.00 p.m. Hughes came back. "I am very sorry but we have had no news back and I doubt if anything will come through tonight Saron. Do you wish to come back tomorrow"? "What, go out

there and chance being killed, I don't
think so, do you"?

"I understand, we have rooms here in the
Embassy, I will get one made up for you,
would you like a sandwich"? "Yes,
please but I am a veggie". "O.K. is
cheese and tomato o.k."? "Yes, thank
you". "O.k. well Sara will take you to
your room and we will bring your food
and a drink up to you".

There was a phone in the room and I
wondered about calling Julie or Helen in
Cornwall but what if Scooby had some
way of finding out and then that
endangers their life? My food and coffee
arrived in my room. Afterwards, I
showered and lay on the bed thinking of
Fabio and how he lost his life because of

me, he never deserved that, he was a good, honest man.

Yes, and you are correct, I will find Scooby and I will kill him for what he did but my immediate problem needs sorting first.

The following day, to my surprise, Sir Clive had apparently been playing golf in Italy, a lucky coincidence, he arrived, shook my hand then proceeded to tell me that I was on my own, that MI6 could not be seen to interfere with the Italian judiciary. To say I lost it was an understatement. "I'll tell you what then, I will go to the Sunday tabloids and tell them everything, even that you can't control your officers because Frank Drake, you probably know him as Frank

Drake, he is a double agent who tried to kill me". You noticed I said is, I didn't want him to know I had killed Drake.

"Look Saron, you may think you can threaten the British Government but you are seriously out of your league, I could quite easily snuff you out here and no questions would be asked so don't try and threaten the service".

"Then what do I do? I just want my life back". "O.k. well now you are being sensible, I can sort you a new passport, get you back to the U.K. and wipe any record of any involvement with MI6". "What about the reason you lot made me join MI6"? "Don't worry. you will start with a new life and a clean slate. I will even have a car left for you at Heathrow.

THE STUNNER 4

So, Saron, it will take a couple of days but everything will be given to Tarquin here". "O.k. I didn't say thank you, I hated the situation his people had put me in and more so the death of my lovely Fabio.

Two days passed and Tarquin came to me and handed me a one-way ticket to Heathrow, a new passport as Saron Leila and a set of car keys for a Fiat 600 and two hundred pounds in sterling.

So, this is it I thought, from now I am on my own and Cornwall beckoned. Maybe Scooby would leave me alone, knowing MI6 were on his case and he now knew I was trained by them.

I guess time will tell on that one I thought as I boarded the plane to Heathrow.

THE STUNNER 4

My little Fiat 600c was waiting for me so I set off for the long drive to Cornwall. I eventually arrived in Polruan and my beautiful cottage. I had decided to go and see Ju and Helen the next day as it was quite late when I arrived and I felt shattered.

I had a great night's sleep, it was so nice to be in my bed and the environment I felt most at ease with. Although I had slept well, I had a little cry over Fabio, I know I will never find another kind, generous man like him. The shame was I didn't have any pictures of him, they were all lost in the horrendous time I had from when he was shot.

The following morning, I sat overlooking Fowey and the beautiful estuary that I

THE STUNNER 4

called home and was thinking how it could have been. I was getting a bit broody, I think my body clock was telling me something.

I showered and put some nice clothes on to go and see my mates, it was now late August so the trade was probably beginning to drop off, or so I thought.

My next shock was about to come. I arrived at the Bistro and it was all boarded up!! I went back into Fowey and got myself a phone and first I called Helen, she said she would get Julie and we could meet at the King of Prussia for lunch and they would explain.

It all seemed mysterious. The pub was quite busy but Ju and Helen were already at the nice table by the window.

THE STUNNER 4

I could see Helen's foot stuck out and as I
got closer, she had a pot on her leg.
"What happened to you"? "It's a long
story" and they poured me a glass of
wine. "You o.k. Ju"? "Not really Saron".
She looked very worried.

"Why is the Bistro shut"? "About three
months ago, we were visited in the
middle of the night by five big, thick-set
men, they had guns Saron. They told us
the Bistro was now shut and if we tried to
re-open, they would kill us and my
family, then they gave us this card, they
said when you surfaced you would have
to ring this number and if the outcome
was satisfactory, we could re-open. What
happened Saron? They said to break the
rules or if you didn't contact this number
then we would never be allowed to open

again. I wanted to get the police involved but Julie was worried about her mum and daughter so I didn't". "Probably the safest thing Helen to be honest, these are really nasty people".

I set about telling them both about everything. "Oh, Saron, that Fabio sounded perfect". "He was Ju, I have never loved a man like that, I heard of true love and I certainly found it". They both said how sorry they were. "Right girls, we have to have a plan, the season is almost over, I have money and can keep you both while I decide how to play Scooby". "Saron, please don't do anything silly". "Ju, Scooby took the most precious thing in my life, Fabio, and that was a big mistake on his part, if I don't cut off the snakes head then I will always be living in fear and I am not doing that, he is arrogant, how dare he affect my friends, his argument is with me, not you two".

"What if he now knows you are back"? "He won't do anything until I contact him". "So, what will you do Saron"? "Don't worry, we will soon be back to normal Ju". I was trying to give them confidence when in reality I wasn't sure how I was going to kill Scooby but I knew I had to.

A month passed and I hardly left the cottage, just in case. I spent my time researching poisons because that was my best bet. I eventually found a simple one, so simple I couldn't believe it. You mixed juice from lupin stems with brown

THE STUNNER 4

sugar which made the juice react then
you boil it slowly for four hours and add
castor oil, apparently what it would do
would make it impossible to pass
anything so the internal organs would
strangulate leaving him dead within four
hours of it being administered. I figured if
I could have a meal with him then apply
poison to his meal or drink. his staff
would be so intent on sorting him I could
slip away.

It was two weeks before Christmas when
I rang the number the girls gave me. A
guy answered and I said who I was, he
immediately handed the phone to Scooby.
"Is this Saron? So lovely to hear from
you, I assume your friends gave you my
message"? "Yes, Scooby, I want to put
this to bed, can we meet"? "Of course, I

always have time for a beautiful woman. Where are you"? "No Scooby, it doesn't work like that. I will meet you at the Caspian restaurant on Bond Street at 8.00 p.m. tomorrow night". "O.k. lady I will be there".

I rang the restaurant, Geo had been a big friend of Luca's, I said I would see him tomorrow afternoon, I had to be sure I could get away and I knew Geo would help me, he had always had a soft spot for me.

I never said anything to the girls, they would only worry. I arrived at the Caspian and told Geo my plan, he was a bit worried that people might think his food had poisoned Scooby. I talked him around, he was too busy looking at my figure. I told him to turn off the CCTV and I gave him the phial of poison, I said to put it into Scooby's brandy that he always drank. Geo was nervous but said Luca had given him the money for the restaurant and would not accept a penny back so he said it was payback time.

This was really going well, I arrived at the same time as Scooby and, like I thought, he had two strong arms with him and they sat at the next table. "Now you have come to see me Saron which I have to say is quite brave, your friend's restaurant can re-open, I am a man of my word". I hated the guy. The waiter came over and handed us menu's, "What would you like to drink"? "A white wine spritzer please", "And for you sir"? "Brandy you bloody fool". Scooby was in one of his, I'm the boss moods, oh how I hated this man He had ordered his brandy, I was now in the hands of Geo.

"So, Saron, you know that I am going to kill you so I asked myself why would you surface again, do you think your looks and figure will save you"? and he laughed, showing his side teeth were gold. "Spritzer for madam and brandy for sir". "It is Napoleon brandy isn't it dumb boy"? "Yes sir, the owner knows what you like".

I said cheers, hoping he would start drinking, the less amount of time I spend with this man the better. "You never answered my question Saron". "I came here to plead for my life Scooby". "Well, you have balls, that is a fact but I'm not sure I can let you go, it's all about standing in the community and you made a fool of me". By now he had drunk about two-thirds of his brandy with no reaction, then suddenly he started holding his throat, his stomach started blowing up. I screamed and the heavies came over and pushed me out of the way, that was my signal, I was gone, leaving that piece of crap writhing in pain and I felt that revenge was mine.

Six hours later I arrived in Polruan. Scooby's death was all over the news channels, they think it has something to do with a foreign country. I was surprised I wasn't mentioned, which was good as there wouldn't have been any CCTV but if they had questioned the other diners then chances are they would have said on the news channels.

I decided to just move on, it's Christmas and time to have some fun. Ju and Helen said they had arranged taxis for us to Padstow, the Swollen Trout had a couple of bands on. I was looking forward to letting my hair down. The girls arrived and we all decided we would go as sexy Santa's.

We walked in the Swollen Trout to quite a few wolf-whistles, I have to say we did look good. Everybody loves Christmas and the three of us were no different, the girls were staying at mine tonight so we could open our presents together and we were cooking dinner together.

THE STUNNER 4

We danced and danced and of course fended off the local lads wanting a female Santa in their stockings. It was almost 1.00 a.m. when we arrived back at the cottage, me and Ju were a bit tipsy, Helen of course opened a bottle of red, for a nightcap she said. Ju went straight to bed. "Just a small glass Helen then I'm going to bed also". "Do you know mate, you are so brave and I'm so pleased we are besties"?

"Me too Helen". "Do you think what you did will mean all the aggravation is over"? "I hope so Helen, I'm trying to push it all to the back of my mind to be honest".

The following morning was fantastic, the tree I had set up with Julie's mum's angel adorning the top was just so magical. We all mucked in doing the meal but obviously, those two were on the turkey whilst I was on the nut roast but the veg was great.

We had Greek salad to start, they had turkey and veg for their main course and I had the nut roast and veg then we had a cheesecake that Helen had made which, of course, had copious amounts of Bailey's in it. We just threw everything in the dishwasher and settled down to watch GREASE for the umpteenth time. Julie loved it. It had almost finished when there was a knock at the door, my heart sank. "Who the hell can that be"? "I don't know Helen, I'd best find out".

THE STUNNER 4

A man and a woman stood at the door. "DI Mark Kaynes and DS Lorna Bright. Sorry to disturb you but I'm afraid you will have to come to London with us as you were having a meal with a gentleman who died at the table in a restaurant".

Oh, crap how do I get out of this I thought. Helen was quite aggressive with the coppers. "Can't you wait just one day? It's bloody Christmas day, don't you lot take a day off"? "It's o.k. Helen, lock up when you two leave tomorrow and take the key with you".

The police escorted me out and we drove to some police station in London. They took me into an interview room. "Would you like a coffee before we start Saron"? "Yes please". I was trying to stay calm running everything through my head so basically just buying time to get my story straight.

"O.k. DS Bright, start the tape. You are sure you don't want legal representation Saron? It is o.k. to call you Saron"? "Yes, that's fine". "O.k. so the man in question was a Mr Caspian Seeburg, how did you know Mr Seeburg"? "I knew from years before". "So, did he get in touch with you and ask you out for a meal"? "Yes, it was a restaurant I liked in London". "O.k. so did you know anything about his business"? "Yes, he had done really well in import and export I believe and was a wealthy man".

"We believe Mr Seeburg was known to the Spanish authorities and MI6 for his dealings in the illegal drug trade". "Caspian selling drugs? I think you may have the wrong person inspector". "I don't think so Saron, we can't be certain yet but we believe he may have been poisoned by a rival gang".

"I'm shocked inspector"!! "What exactly happened"? "Well, we sat down and ordered our food then we were talking about old times and he suddenly fell backwards, then two guys on the next table tried to help, I was so upset". "So, upset you left almost straight away"? "No, that's not correct, they pronounced him dead and that's when I left, I assumed he'd had a massive heart attack, there was nothing I could do, they took him away". I knew they had no CCTV footage so couldn't have known if I had stayed.

"Interesting Saron, why did you assume it was a heart attack"? "Well, wasn't it"? "In your own words, what made you think that"? "Well, he was holding his throat and clutching his chest so I assumed. Why, do you know different"? "Yes, we do, Mr Seeburg was poisoned but as yet we don't know how, we believe it could be a killing from another country and we are looking into that. Did he have links with Russia"? "I couldn't tell you, we only spoke socially".

"The poison used is not known by our scientists and because you met and I am sure possibly embraced, we would like you to take a simple test". Now I was bricking it, what if they found any residue on me? "Oh, o.k. do you think I am in danger"? I said, playing little Miss innocent for all it was worth.

DI Kayne called in a doctor, he took a blood sample then Kayne said it was in my interest to stay at the station overnight until the results came through.

That night in the cell, well, cell the door was open, I wasn't exactly locked up, my head was spinning, I think I might have got away with this I thought.

The following morning, they brought me tea and toast and then I was called back into the interview room. "So, Saron, not great news to be honest, we have found a very slight trace of the poison in your blood".

My heart sank. "Our people don't think it has had any effect on you and you will pass it naturally and may already have done so but, that aside, it does throw a different light on the case". "What do you mean"? "Well, with your permission, we would like to arrange a search of your house in Cornwall". "Oh, I'm not sure about that with me being here". "Well, that's just it, we intend to hold you for a further forty-eight hours, pending the outcome of a search, which we can obtain a court order for, or, to move things quicker, you can just give us your permission".

"It doesn't sound like you are giving me much choice". "So, is that a yes then Sharon"? "O.k." "We will also need to keep you under surveillance because of the poison found in your bloodstream".

Another day sat in a bloody prison cell, I was just hoping they didn't find anything at the house.

I was playing what I did over and over in my head so it was fingers crossed I guess.

The following day, it was late afternoon, when I was taken into the interview room again, but this time it was just me and DI Mark Kayne. "So, Saron, looking at what the Cornwall police have reported, the case has gone to another level. We have basically been told to hand you over to MI6". "What? This is crazy". "They will be here in a minute, do you want a coffee"? "Yes, please".

THE STUNNER 4

A few minutes passed and a guy came in with DI Kayne. "Saron Leila? I'm Manson Eagle, MI6" and he produced his warrant card. "O.K. DI Kayne, you can leave Miss Leila with me now, she is under our jurisdiction".

"What the hell is going on"? "Just stay calm Saron, we, that is MI6, have just saved your bacon, you would be up for murder now otherwise, you don't have to come with me, you can leave with me then go straight home, that is your choice but we would be duty-bound to inform the Police of your decision and then you can take your chances".

"So, basically I don't have a choice, so what now"? "Well, I will take you over to

THE STUNNER 4

MI6 and we will tell you what we want in return".

Manson Eagle drove a silver Range Rover Sport and didn't hang about, we were soon at MI6 Headquarters. I was shown into another room where I sat for over an hour before Sir Gavin Clearmont came in and sat opposite me.

"Oh, dear Saron, we really did get in a pickle didn't we, Miss Natural Born killer". I just looked intensely at him. "You see Saron, as much as I let you leave the secret service, we never leave our people, they are always MI6, and you are no different".

"That's bullshit, I have murdered the one guy you wanted off your books". "Great analogy Saron but Seeburg, or Scooby as you knew him, you killed before we could get all the intelligence we needed to shut down his operations and now his crazy half-brother, Patrice Amir is running operations, this guy is a complete psycho and, to that end, we have to take him down, and that's where you come in".

"Now hang on a minute, we had a deal". "Yes, we did. I was more than fair sorting it out for you but you decided to go back for a second bite, didn't you"? "Look, he killed the only man I ever loved". "Oh, yes, Mr. Fabio, well I won't spoil your illusion Saron".

"What are you implying"? "Nothing to bother yourself about, I'm sure it will all come out one day". "No, tell me". "I am not at liberty to say but you dear, now have to make a decision, because you went against the rules we need you to infiltrate Patrice Amir's outfit". "That's o.k. but what about the two heavies that were with Scooby in the restaurant"? "Don't worry about them, they are, shall we say, no longer with us. So now, you travel on your own passport, and we will reissue you a gun, your contact in Malta will be Agent Eagle".

"What do I need to do"? "Weekly, you will meet with Manson Eagle and report everything you find out" "And how the hell am I supposed to do that"? "You work that out but there won't be another chance so you'd better come good, or they will throw the key away". He gave me a picture of Patrice and told me where he drank and the restaurants he frequented and there was a return ticket to Malta and a promise after this that it would all be over.

I was certainly going to play this differently, just get the info they require and no confrontation, no killing, just purely that.

The flight to Malta from Stansted wasn't too long and we touched down, armed with the name of the hotel, which made me smile "The Jolly Fisherman" and it had a big picture of that logo from Skegness, I only visited once with Girl Guides and vowed never to go again.

The guy on reception was the owner, he was about mid-fifties and seemed a nice guy but he was intent on telling me that he was from Skegness and moved over here and bought this hotel eight years ago. At least he was English I thought. "Breakfast is 7.00 a.m. to 9.30 a.m. and evening meal, if you require, one, you have to book before 5.00 p.m. for either the 7.30 p.m. or the 8.00 p.m. sitting, and it gets very busy". Now, I'm not being a snobby cow but meat and potato pie, chips, carrots and peas with lashings of gravy really aren't for me. I thanked him, he said his name was Tony Curtis, his mother had a crush on the film star and because their surname was Curtis, she named him Tony.

I can assure you he was nothing like bloody Tony Curtis, more like Woody out of Toy Story I thought!!

THE STUNNER 4

Anyway, I slept o.k. that night, other than thinking the girls would be worried about me but there was nothing I could do.

I spent the next day wandering around the island, it was quite pleasantly warm, not too hot and the people were very friendly, apparently something to do with the Second World War. One of the bars Patrice frequented was called The Florin, it was a Maltese bar, you could have a drink or like a Tapas selection.

I dressed as seductively as I dared in the hope that Patrice might come in. I was in there at 7.30 p.m. and was just about to give up when he came swaggering in, he had on a suit and a beige camel coat over his shoulders like some kind of Mafia boss. He sat at the bar and just clicked his

THE STUNNER 4

fingers, and a young waitress came running. He ordered some Tapas and a Long Island iced tea, he wasn't with anybody, that told me he felt safe and didn't need bodyguards.

I was at the end of a long bar but leaned forward to catch the barman's attention and to show some cleavage toward Patrice, I clocked he had spotted me. "Large Hendricks, spot of lime and a slice of cucumber". I'll get the pretty girl that". "Well, thank you", this was my opportunity so I wandered down the bar. "Would you mind if I joined you"? "No, by all means, that would be very nice".

He seemed quite charming, we swapped names, then mobile numbers and he asked if I fancied a meal on Saturday night. He said he knew a lovely little restaurant called Sovarious, he asked if he could pick me up at 7.30 p.m. on Saturday night. I didn't want to sound too keen but said, if you wish.

He really didn't seem like the psycho that he was painted as by MI6, but we will see. With three days to spare, I wandered around the streets and was impressed with the little coffee houses adorning the town and the friendly nature of the people.

I sat daydreaming at one of the coffee houses thinking about mum and dad and how they would have loved the friendly people and the architecture of the town.

Eventually, Saturday came around and I wore my tight-fitting red dress with black stockings and black Christian Le Boutin high heels. Though I say it myself, I don't half scrub up well, as dad used to say.

He picked me up in a classic Mercedes Cabriolet, his face when I got in the car made me realise, I had him on the hook. We drove to the North of the Island to the restaurant which I believed was a traditional Maltese one.

They knew Patrice, in fact, they seemed in awe of him, or maybe frightened of him, I wasn't sure but he seemed o.k. to me. The menu was all Maltese but they had an excellent vegetarian menu and I had a camembert roulade with crusty bread and for my main, I had quail egg and creme fresh salad which was excellent. I asked Patrice what he did and

he openly told me, drug smuggling,
which took me back, to say the least. I
told him I was on a fashion shoot which,
looking at the way he was looking at me,
it was easy to pull off.

The night was going well but, just as we
were about to leave, a young waiter came
over with the bill. He looked at it and
asked the guy what was it? "Sorry sir, is
it incorrect"? He grabbed the guy. "You
bet it is" and he grabbed and stuffed the
bill in his mouth. I was shocked, he
looked at me menacingly, "Come on" and
he grabbed my arm roughly. Now I had
seen the menacing side of the man. Back
in the car, it was like a switch had been
flipped, he was the perfect gentleman
again. I knew from that point how

dangerous this probably was going to be for me.

Although he had pretty much been ogling me all night, and I expected an awkward situation before he dropped me off, it was nothing of the kind, he thanked me for a nice evening and said he would be in touch.

The next few days I treated like it was a holiday but decided I needed to call Manson Eagle. He said we could meet and the English Homestead Café in the square at 11.00 a.m.

To be fair, Manson seemed a decent guy once I got to know him. He told me a lot about Patrice and the things he was alleged to have done but he said the whole of Malta was afraid of him and his people so he pretty much did as he pleased. He also said I should never go to the Police as Patrice had the Chief of Police Patrice and the judges in his pocket.

I told him I had made contact and what he had done in the restaurant. He said the waiter was lucky to be alive as he would have thought nothing of shooting the poor man.

The comment from Clearmont about Fabio had played on my mind so I decided that, as we were getting along so well, I would take a chance to ask about the comment.

Manson looked at me. "Come on Manson, what was that all about"? "O.K., but you didn't hear it from me. Fabio was a partner in crime with the guy you knew as Scooby". "No, that's not right, he told me he use to own an engineering company, he told me about his wife and I met their friends"." All fake Saron, eventually he would have traded you, it was his life or yours. We intercepted a telephone call he made where he said he would find you and hand you over and the agreement was he would then have repaid his debt to Scooby".

I sat gobsmacked, yet again, a man had made a fool of me. I just couldn't believe it, this man was so kind and generous, all the things a girl dreams of in a man.

After leaving Manson I walked back to the hotel feeling very down that the man I had finally given my heart to was actually just going to use me as a trading piece to save his own skin. I can't pretend to tell you how low I felt. I really wanted to call the girls but knew I couldn't.

My heart really wasn't in this for MI6, and I wondered about just going on the run, but that would mean I had thrown my life away. Mum used to say, what goes around comes around, maybe this was my time to be paid back. I sat on the end of the bed and cried and cried. Yes, me, Saron, that confident girl you have read about. I can hear you screaming at me "Get a grip Saron, you are the Stunner"

The following morning, with very red and sore eyes, I went for my breakfast at the hotel. Tony Curtis was taking the orders, there were three other people there, he was joking with them, they were from Liverpool and the woman in the group I swear was Cilla Blacks twin sister, she even sounded like her. Eventually Tony Curtis came over to take my order. "Good morning, Saron, what can I do for you"? I was thinking perhaps shut up would be a start. "Black coffee and a poached egg on toast please". "Would you like some English bacon with that"? "No, thank you, I'm a vegetarian". "Did you hear that Scouse? We have a leftie in our midst"! and he laughed and flounced off.

Once breakfast was over, I went back to my room, I really could not understand why Fabio would have done that to me, it certainly wasn't the Fabio I knew and loved. I was still very full of emotion when my mobile rang. "Saron, it's Patrice, I wish for you to come to my pool party on Saturday night, if you say yes, I will send my driver to pick you up at 6.00 p.m."

"Oh, yes Patrice, that would be nice". "O.k. I will see you Saturday" and he hung up. I rang Manson Eagle and told him about the party. "That's good Saron, I think a lot of his business associates will be there so if you can mingle and try to remember names that would be great. I can put a wire on you if you wish"? "No, not yet, let me build their trust first".

I had come out of my depressed state by the time Saturday came around and maybe I was destined to always fall for the bad boys.

Patrice sent a guy to pick me up he was dressed in chauffer gear and driving a Bentley Arnage. I wore some loose-fitting clothes with my favourite red bikini underneath. Arriving at this beautiful house right on the headland there was every kind of flash car parked at the house and the party was in full swing.

There were loads of pretty girls in bikinis and girls serving the drinks and nibbles. "Saron, lovely to see you" and Patrice kissed me on the cheek, "Come and meet my good friend Argar Whiteley, he has been a close business associate of mine for many years.

THE STUNNER 4

Argar, this is the beautiful Saron, she is doing a photoshoot". I had to think quickly. "Oh, I have finished the shoot". "What was the magazine it was for"? I was guessing Argar knew somebody in the photoshoot game because his interest was more than just a passing interest.

"Oh, it was for holiday brochures, you know me and a guy running out of the sea type". "The reason I ask Saron is because I know the head of the licensing authority who arranges permits". The pretty girl stood with him whispered something in his ear. "Sorry, my girlfriend just pointed out he was sacked six months ago for inappropriate behaviour toward a colleague". I felt a sigh of relief. "So how long are you staying in Malta"? "Oh, I have another shoot in Sweden in three weeks so I think I will stop until then".

Argar then just turned and started discussing business with Patrice. I was trying to listen but Olivia, his girlfriend, kept talking. I did hear Argar say Patrice would need ten or twelve men to carry the cartons of drugs so that the boat could get away before the coastguard came and caught them at Golden Bay. "It's midnight, Tuesday Patrice, the supplier is insisting you are there with the men, he said he has a proposition for you". "O.k. I'll be there".

The night was quite pleasant and I was chuffed with the information I could pass on the next time I saw Manson. I was just about to leave when it kicked off, Patrice had a swarthy looking guy by the throat, he had spilt a drink in the pool and was laughing about it. I asked Olivia who he was, she said Dimitri the Greek. "Is he a friend of Patrice"? "Yes, he is in charge of all the security". I just acted dumb.

"Tell Patrice goodnight and thanks for a nice evening" and I left. The following day I couldn't wait to talk with Manson so he arranged for us to meet at the coffee shop again.

We sat at the back so that we weren't too much on show. "O.k. Manson, I think what I am about to tell you should release me totally to go back to my normal life, if not then I'm not prepared to give you this information or it will be obvious where it came from". "I can't sanction that, it's way above my pay grade Saron". "O.k. then we meet tomorrow after you have spoken with Clearmont but time is running out. I want a flight back to the U.K. tomorrow night and total immunity from any further prosecution and I want it signing by Clearmont himself". "Wow, you must have something Saron". I got up, looked at Manson and said, "Tomorrow, 10.00 a.m. here" and I walked out. I took a steady stroll around the streets taking my time window shopping, I was feeling quite pleased with the thought that I may soon have my life back.

That night I had a nice meal looking over the bay, a couple of glasses of red wine then headed for bed happy in the knowledge I could be free to enjoy my life. That night I dreamt about Fabio, it was like he was with me, he was so kind and gentle like he was looking over me.

The following morning, I was met by two men in suits, they showed their credentials and said they needed to get me out of Malta that morning. "What are you on about"? "Sir Gavin Clearmont will meet you at the airport".

It was all a whirlwind but genuine from what I could make out. I came out onto the concourse and Clearmont was waiting, he whisked me to headquarters for what he said was a debriefing.

"Coffee Saron"? "Yes please, you do know that's it for you people"? Clearmont just smiled and returned a few minutes later with a folder stuffed with papers and a coffee each. "So, Saron, please tell me what you know". "Only when I get the signed piece of paper from you". Clearmont reached into the folder and handed me an envelope. I opened it and it was on official paper, basically relinquishing me from any future MI6 missions and any prosecution from any historic previous criminal activities.

Wow, I thought this is going well. "So, Sir Gavin, I'd best tell you what I know. I went to Patrice Amir's house to a pool party and he openly talked about his drug dealing. He had another associate who was equally arrogant to talk openly, they talked and I listened. Patrice and Argar Whiteley, I think he is the actual smuggler who brings the drugs into Malta and then they are distributed from there.

THE STUNNER 4

There is a shipment coming in on Tuesday night at Golden Bay and Argar said Patrice must be there with about twelve men because a new deal was to be discussed also".

"This is excellent work". "Tell me Sir Gavin, what if they work out it was me"? "Don't worry, we look after our own which in the very near future you will find out but, in-between times, we have mocked up your suicide and it's been shown on Maltese television so as far as these gangs are concerned, you are history".

This was all better than I could have hoped for, the only bit I wasn't understanding was when he said they looked after his own and I would find out

THE STUNNER 4

in the future but, to be honest, I just
wanted to get home and knowing now
they had faked my death in Malta was a
great feeling, funny as that may sound.

THE STUNNER 4

Chapter 11

On the drive to Cornwall, I was thinking I would treat the girls to a week's holiday somewhere hot before deciding what I wanted in my life. I had that money in the bank and I had my beautiful cottage in Polruan so onwards and upwards.

On the way down, I phoned Julie and she said let's meet at Rick Steins in Padstow for a meal the following night.

Now you may think that is the end of things so far but, as usual, another twist was waiting, I'll leave you to try and figure that one out.

My little cottage was a little damp so I set to getting the log burner going and it was soon all warm and cosy.

THE STUNNER 4

The following night I headed for Padstow and the famous Rick Steins restaurant. Julie and Helen were already there. Big hugs all around and we sat with a glass of champagne and I told them about Fabio and how I had been conned, then about MI6 and my arranged death. I told them how much I loved Fabio and can't believe he betrayed me, I had never totally given anyone my heart until him.

They both listened but then stood up and said have a lovely evening and they would speak tomorrow. "What? Where are you going"? There was a tap on my shoulder, I turned around and it was Fabio, I almost fainted, by now the girls had gone. "You are dead". "Not quite Saron, may I"? and he took a seat opposite me. He then told me the full

THE STUNNER 4

story, that they had tracked Patrice for four years and every time they got close, he was one step ahead. "They eventually realised they must have a double agent who had also worked with Frank, who you got rid of Frank and Manson worked for Scooby, hence the story Manson gave you. We realised all this, mine and your meeting, wasn't just luck, it was planned. The guy who shot me worked for us, there were no live bullets in his gun.

The problem we had was, we had to keep the deceit going and we believe when we pulled you out that Manson had informed Patrice that there was something dodgy about you. So, I insisted we got you out and faked your death".

             282

THE STUNNER 4

"So, all this about a wife and an engineering company wasn't true"? "The wife was true, she was a very rich lady, when we married, she wanted me to leave MI6. Sir Gavin agreed but only on the understanding that, if they needed me, I would help out. I said I would and that day, meeting you, I was having a great life, he knew I had a boat so MI6 set it all up.

I am sorry I lied to you but I was determined to be with you and the only way was to stick it through and once we had the information, I insisted they fake your death so that we could have a safe life together, if you still want me"?

"Of course, I do, I love you, Fabio. How come Julie and Helen were involved"?

THE STUNNER 4

"I was concerned you might not talk to me so I met with them yesterday, told them the full story and said if our stories didn't match then I would walk away, if they did, I told Helen to give me a sign and I would come over".

"Wow, even my besties are secret agents now"! and I laughed. We had a lovely meal then drove back to Polruan with my love and my second chance at happiness.

He absolutely loved the cottage in Polruan and, of course, the benefits we had both missed, as he carried me into the bedroom.

He was so kind and gentle, his only concern was for me whilst we made love. You can imagine it was soon over, it had been some time for us plus all the emotion came out of me and I cried but only with happiness that he was back in my life again.

The following day, we met Julie and Helen for drinks and to my surprise they had a couple of guys in tow. Julie said she met Tom at a computer skills class they were both doing. Tom apparently was setting up an online store selling to Brits abroad, you know, Tetley tea, McVities chocolate digestives, all that stuff. Tom was quite loud for Julie but maybe that's what she needed. Helen, on the other hand, had met an ex-army guy called John who appeared to be down on his luck, he said he was between jobs which would have sent alarm bells to me but, if she is happy then I am.

THE STUNNER 4

Tom wanted to know everything about MI6 but, of course, Fabio couldn't divulge anything, or me for that matter but he kept probing. Fabio handled it very well then to my complete surprise, in the middle of the pub, he dropped on one knee and produced a beautiful diamond and emerald ring. He uttered those magical words "Will you marry me Saron"? Tears just rolled down my cheeks. "Of course, I will my darling". It's a weird feeling because I had never thought about being married, not ever and here I was accepting a proposal.

The girls shrieked with delight and ran around and hugged me while Tom and John just looked bemused, I'm not sure they knew what they had let themselves in for.

THE STUNNER 4

The following day Fabio was busy making arrangements and managed to get a booking at St Ednoc's Church on Rock, this was an absolutely beautiful setting and I was so excited. Helen organized a hen night and the girls from London were coming and stopping the week so they could attend the wedding.

Listen to me talking about weddings, who would have thought that? There was a beautiful wedding dress shop in St Mawes so me and the girls went there for my dress and their dresses. Fabio had asked an old work colleague who he called Smithy to be his best man so everything was set.

I wanted the girls to have dark blue dresses and I chose an off the shoulder

THE STUNNER 4

number which was actually a mini skirt and it had a long train.

On Thursday, Penny and Andrea, the London girls, arrived and of course, we had loads to catch up on. They were such lovely girls and have always been good friends. We had decided to spend the night in St Ives and ended up in the Pink Coconut. Helen was on top form and it was a foregone conclusion I would be ill the next day as, at the very first pub she ordered drinks and shots of Tennessee whisky which, to be honest, was quite moorish. By the time we arrived at the Pink Coconut, I was at that stage where I thought, to hell with tomorrow, let's party!

THE STUNNER 4

Five pretty girls hitting the dance floor caused quite a stir. I know Penny and Andrea, who were not in any relationships, were certainly having a good time. Our taxi picked us up at 1.00 a.m. and we dropped Ju and Helen off at theirs and Penny and Andrea were stopping at mine.

The following morning, I felt so ill with a hangover. The other girls didn't seem too bad. Penny was sat with her muesli and Greek yoghurt, Andrea with her cornflakes and me sat with my head in my hands and a drink of Alka Seltzer!

That day was a total wipeout for me but by Friday I felt a lot better and ready for my big day, we had chosen Glarins restaurant on Rock for the reception, it

THE STUNNER 4

was a two-star Michelin restaurant, because there was just a small party of us, we thought that would be nice.

People who go to Cornwall never go across to Rock and it really is a lovely place. I arrived at the church, Tom was giving me away I know what you are thinking gobby, Tom!! Well, my choices were limited. They had decorated the front entrance to the church with blue and white flowers adorning the entrance archway.

I felt like a princess, the girls looked fabulous in their blue dresses. It was soon done and, to be honest, I know it sounds a bit cheesy but I didn't want the day to end.

THE STUNNER 4

I did have one small shock Fabio's best man was none other than Matthew who I had met and was to be my contact if you remember with Paris? Anyway, it didn't matter, he was very discreet, Fabio said they joined MI6 together. I have to say there is so much crosstalk and unknowns in the Secret Service, I was glad I wasn't in it anymore.

At the reception the food was unbelievable. Julie had secretly made the wedding cake which again was fabulous Everybody did their speeches and of course, Tom droned on and on until we had to tell him to sit down and let Matthew do his best man speech.

"First of all, can I say how honoured I am to be Fabio's best man? We have been friends for many years and so it's best I make sure he is squirming in his seat" and he laughed.

"If there's anybody here today who's feeling nervous, apprehensive and queasy at the thought of what lies ahead, it's probably because you've just married Fabio. It's been a wonderful and emotional day, even the cake is in tiers, lovely cake by the way, made by the beautiful Julie, let's give Julie a round of applause for that.

I did ask for a microphone but was told one wasn't available so if you can't hear me at the back, the silence from the people at the front should reassure you that you're not missing out on anything.

THE STUNNER 4

When Fabio asked me to be his best man, I asked what it entailed. He told me I can't get away with a few thank-you's and a quick toast in this speech. Apparently, as best man, I'm supposed to sing the groom's praises and talk about his good qualities. Unfortunately, I can't sing and I won't lie. No, seriously though, Fabio is a lovely guy. It's strange giving a speech like this, my parents always said if I had nothing nice to say about anyone then say nothing!!

For those of you that don't know me, my name is Matthew or Matt, my friends call me by my full name though which is, Matt Would -you - like-a -drink? If you don't mind if

you are talking to me at the bar, I
would appreciate you using my full
name.

 I'm going to wrap it up now but
before I finish, the manager of this
beautiful establishment has asked
me to tell you that, for Health and
Safety reasons, please don't get on
the tables or chairs for my standing
ovation.

Raise your glasses to a lovely couple
Saron and Fabio".

We had a lovely evening and I
didn't want to let my new husband
out of my sight. I felt like the
luckiest girl in the whole world.

THE STUNNER 4

The following day, Fabio had booked us to go to Cuba for two weeks, a man full of surprises, I guess only time will tell if my happiness lasts so, until next time.

Sometimes, people come into our lives and quickly go. Some stay for a while in your life and leave footprints on your heart and you are never the same again. Until next time   *Love Saron x*

THE STUNNER 4

Thank you to all my loyal readers. The Stunner, the first in the series, was going to be a one-off but, due to such high demand of my readers wanting a follow up, I set about Stunner Two then Stunner Three came along now the release of Stunner Four.

It's been a massive pleasure writing the series and hopefully, you will have enjoyed all the books. So, as Saron says, until next time my friends.

Colin H Galtrey
AUTHOR

THE STUNNER 4

If you have enjoyed this book, take a look at the full catalogue available in Paperback and Kindle on Amazon/Goodreads Book Bub to name a few also many now on Audio at Amazon/Audible.com and I Tunes

Visit my website

www.colingaltrey.co.uk

Facebook page Colin J Galtrey Author

Instagram: thepeakdistrict author

THE STUNNER 4

Printed in Great Britain
by Amazon